THIS GAME
OF WAR

THIS GAME OF WAR

ED BUTTS

RONSDALE PRESS

THIS GAME OF WAR
Copyright © 2022 Ed Butts

RONSDALE PRESS
3350 West 21st Avenue, Vancouver, B.C. Canada V6S 1G7
www.ronsdalepress.com

Typesetting: Julie Cochrane, in Minion 12 pt on 16
Cover Design: Julie Cochrane
Paper: Rolland Enviro Print 60 lb.

Ronsdale Press wishes to thank the following for their support of its
publishing program: the Canada Council for the Arts, the Government of
Canada, the British Columbia Arts Council, and the Province of British
Columbia through the British Columbia Book Publishing Tax Credit program.

Library and Archives Canada Cataloguing in Publication

Title: This game of war / Ed Butts.
Names: Butts, Edward, 1951– author.
Identifiers: Canadiana (print) 2022027908X | Canadiana (ebook) 20220279101
    | ISBN 9781553806837 (softcover) | ISBN 9781553806844 (HTML) | ISBN
    9781553806851 (PDF)
Classification: LCC PS8603.U88 T55 2022 | DDC jC813/.6—dc23

At Ronsdale Press we are committed to protecting the environment. To this
end we are working with Canopy and printers to phase out our use of paper
produced from ancient forests. This book is one step towards that goal.

Printed in Canada.

For my father, Edward Joseph "Ted" Butts,
and my mother, Patricia Marjory Butts
(née Bidwell), veterans of World War II

In memory of my nephew,
Cameron Joseph Kulnies

IN FLANDERS FIELDS

In Flanders fields the poppies blow
Between the crosses, row on row,
That mark our place; and in the sky
The larks, still bravely singing, fly
Scarce heard amid the guns below.

We are the Dead. Short days ago
We lived, felt dawn, saw sunset glow,
Loved, and were loved, and now we lie
        In Flanders fields.

Take up our quarrel with the foe:
To you from failing hands we throw
The torch; be yours to hold it high.
If ye break faith with us who die
We shall not sleep, though poppies grow
        In Flanders fields.

JOHN MCCRAE

1
Teddy's Plan

TEDDY COULDN'T WAIT for the 3:30 bell. *Every* Friday afternoon, he watched the clock on the classroom wall and counted the minutes until he'd be free for the weekend. But this Friday afternoon, he was especially anxious to get out of school and hurry home so he could study his *Official War Games Strategy Book*. The next day, the Super Comics Store at the mall would be hosting the biggest War Games competition that had ever come to town. The best players in town would be there. Teddy was a master at War Games, and he wanted to get in on the action. However, he'd have to show up early to secure a place at a table.

This particular Friday afternoon was especially long. His

grade-eight teacher, Ms. Potts, had introduced the class to Mr. Sanderson, a veteran of the Korean War. She had made sure the students had poppies pinned on before he arrived. Dressed in his uniform, Mr. Sanderson told the class about his experiences in the Royal Canadian Air Force. He allowed the students to pass his military medals around so they could have a good look at them. Teddy was bored and so distracted by clock-watching that when his friend Paul passed a medal to him, he dropped it.

The *clink* of the medal hitting the floor jarred Teddy back to attention. Before he could say, "Sorry," Ms. Potts snapped, "Teddy Nugent! Eyes off the clock! Please pick up Mr. Sanderson's medal and pass it to Valerie, and then apologize to Mr. Sanderson."

Teddy blushed from embarrassment as the other kids snickered. Paul whispered, "Good one, Tedder."

Valerie gave Teddy that look of hers that made him feel like his pants had fallen down. As he handed her the medal, she rolled her eyes and let out an impatient little *huff* that meant she thought he was a bonehead. Teddy liked Valerie a lot.

"I'm very sorry, Mr. Sanderson," Teddy said. "It just slipped."

"Well, we all make slips, don't we?" Mr. Sanderson replied. "You know what, Teddy? When I was given that medal, I was really nervous. But the man who had to pin it on me was even more nervous. He dropped it, too. He was a general, so you're in good company."

Paul said, "General Teddy," and the class laughed.

The bell finally rang. Mr. Sanderson thanked Ms. Potts and her students for having him as their guest and then left. On any ordinary Friday, the kids would have grabbed their backpacks and headed for the door and weekend freedom. This time, Ms. Potts called out, "One minute, please!"

Teddy thought, *Oh, for . . . Now what!*

Ms. Potts said, "Just in case anyone needs a reminder, tomorrow is November 11 and you're expected to be at school by nine o'clock. School buses will take you to the arena for the Remembrance Day ceremony. Now, I know *it's Saturday*, and you'd like to be doing other things. But Mr. Sanderson has just given us some very good reasons to remember why we should all be there. It's just a couple of hours out of your time."

Teddy had already made up his mind that he *wouldn't* be there. He'd be getting a jump on the lineup for a place in the War Games competition. Then Ms. Potts made an announcement that threatened to crush his plan.

"Your homework assignment is to write a composition about your thoughts on the ceremony. It's to be handed in first thing Monday morning."

Seriously! Teddy thought. *How can she do this to me? Time for a little War Games-type strategy.* He had a plan worked out by the time he started walking home with Paul and Valerie.

"I think Mr. Sanderson made up that story about the

general dropping the medal just so you wouldn't feel so bad about having butterfingers," Paul said.

Paul had been joking about Teddy dropping the medal ever since they got out of school. That didn't bother Teddy, because he and Paul kidded around all the time. But Valerie didn't think it was so funny.

"That medal is very important to Mr. Sanderson," she said. "You should've been more respectful."

Teddy was annoyed that Valerie was lecturing him the way Ms. Potts would. A guy expected his teacher to get on his case sometimes. But Valerie . . . well . . . he didn't want *her* to be annoyed with him.

"I didn't *mean* to drop the stupid medal!" he blurted. "And I'm *not* going to the stupid Remembrance Day *thing* that is the *same stupid thing* every year!"

"Teddy, you *have* to go," Valerie said. "I *want* to go. Especially after hearing Mr. Sanderson. Weren't you even paying attention?"

Paul laughed and said, "War Games competition at the mall tomorrow. That's what he was thinking about, weren't you Tedder?"

Valerie stopped walking and said, "*What!* That *dumb* game? Seriously! You're skipping Remembrance Day for *that*? Teddy, you are such a *child*!"

As soon as Paul heard her say that word, he stopped laughing and knew he'd better shut up. But the word stung Teddy.

"*Seriously?*" he said. "I'm a *child*? This is only the biggest

War Games competition this town has ever had. Give me a break!"

Valerie rolled her eyes and let out that huff. Paul said he remembered he had a granola bar in his backpack and started digging for it. Teddy kept talking because *he* was getting mad.

"It's the same thing every year," he complained. "They have a ceremony at the arena. People make boring speeches while other people play noisy bagpipes, shoot guns, and sing 'In Flanders Fields.' Then everybody leaves. Same thing over and over again! What's the point? *Who cares?* Those wars are all old history."

"You can't get out of it," Valerie said.

"Yeah. They'll be taking attendance," Paul said. "Hey! I found it! Chocolate chip! Anybody want a bite?" He held up a granola bar that looked half squashed.

"How many years has that been in your backpack, Paul?" Valerie asked, shaking her head.

Teddy wasn't interested in Paul's granola bar. "Oh, I'll be at school for attendance," he said. "And I'll go to the arena on the bus. When we get there, I'll just *looose* myself in the crowd going in."

He made a sly look as he drew the word out and made air quotes with his fingers. "Then I'll slip out a side entrance and head for the mall. Easy-peasy!"

"*Lemon-squeezy!*" said Paul. "Gotta say the whole thing!"

"Paul, just eat your stale old bar while I try to talk sense to this child," Valerie ordered.

"Got it!" Paul said. He knew better than to argue when Valerie had *that* tone in her voice.

Valerie said, "Teddy, Ms. Potts will see that you're missing. She'll ask you about it on Monday. *Then* what will you do?"

"I've got that covered," Teddy said with a self-satisfied grin. "I'll tell her I had to go to the washroom. You know, stomach ache! Had to be in there for a long time. When I came out — well, the arena was packed with thousands of kids. I couldn't find our class, and things had already started, so I just watched with the people up in the standing room area. And *then*, if she asks why I wasn't on the bus back to school, I'll say I got caught in the crowd and missed it, so I just went home on a city bus. Pretty clever, huh?"

"Pretty *stupid*!" Valerie said. "You'll get caught and be in extra trouble for lying to Ms. Potts. You'll be in trouble with your parents, too. They'll probably ground you until Christmas."

"I won't get caught!" Teddy argued. He really wished Valerie would say his plan was cool, even brilliant. He thought it would be great if she'd sneak off with him and watch him wipe out the competition at War Games. It would be great if Paul came, too, and . . . No. For this stunt, just him and Valerie. But he knew she'd never go for it. Not Valerie.

"It won't be *all* lies, because I really will go home on a city bus — from the mall."

He was ready with an answer when Paul asked, "What about the homework? You can't write it if you're not there."

"City cable news," Teddy said. "I can watch the whole boring Remembrance Day thing online. And you guys can fill me in, too, right? You know, in case something weird happens."

"Yeah!" Paul said. "Like if I let a big fart just when they fire the guns?"

"*Child!*" Valerie said, with rolling eyes and a huff.

When Teddy left them at a street corner, Valerie was still lecturing Paul about the very idea of letting one go during the Remembrance Day ceremony. "*Sooo* disrespectful!" she chided. But now Teddy put that out of mind. He was already plotting War Games tactics.

Teddy stopped at a convenience store a block from his house to buy a snack. He always liked to have a little something to munch on while doing homework — or studying his War Games book. An elderly woman was ahead of him at the counter. Teddy looked around while she rummaged through her purse for money, his gaze going from the candy bar shelf to the newspaper rack to the big round mirror in a top corner of the room.

The mirror gave Mr. Singh, the man behind the counter, a view of most of the store's interior. But at that moment, Mr. Singh was busy helping the customer in front of him. Teddy stuck his tongue out at his own reflection. Then he almost dropped his bag of chips and bottle of juice.

The Teddy looking back at him had his tongue stuck out but wasn't dressed in a Toronto Maple Leafs cap, black and brown jacket, blue jeans and running shoes. That Teddy was wearing some kind of army uniform! It was *him* alright, but how . . .

Then the reflection was normal again. Store aisles and cooler doors, the older woman and Mr. Singh. And Teddy in cap, jacket, jeans and shoes — with his tongue stuck out and his eyes looking like they were about to pop out of his head. Teddy pulled his tongue back in and the Teddy in the mirror did, too. Teddy closed one eye. So did mirror Teddy. *Of course, you bonehead*, Teddy thought. *It's a mirror.*

The woman paid for her purchases, which Mr. Singh put in a bag. She turned around and said, "I know you, Teddy Nugent." She was looking him right in the eye.

Surprised, Teddy could only manage to say, "Excuse me?"

The woman said, "Accept the poppy." Then she left the store. The bell above the door jingled.

Teddy was bewildered. The woman was a stranger to him. But she must know him from somewhere. How else would she know his name? Maybe she was a friend of his parents he'd met once and then forgotten about. But why did she say, "Accept the poppy"? A little box of poppies was on the counter beside the cash register, but Teddy already had one, so why should he buy another?

After paying for his chips and juice, Teddy pointed to the mirror and said, "Mr. Singh, is that a trick mirror?"

"Oh yes," the storekeeper replied. "It's a good trick on any kids who try to pocket candy bars when they think I can't see them."

The idea of stealing candy bars had never once entered Teddy's head. "No, that's not what I mean. Is it, like, *computerized* to do things like . . . Photoshop reflections?"

"That's the same old mirror that's always been up there, Teddy," Mr. Singh said. "What are you talking about?"

"Well, I saw . . ." Teddy stopped without finishing his sentence. Mr. Singh might think he was crazy if he said what he *thought* he saw.

"Um, nothing," Teddy said as he stuffed his items into his backpack. "Thanks very much, Mr. Singh. Bye."

Teddy went out the door, still wondering just *what* he had seen. He was about to head home when a voice said, "Want a poppy, son?"

Teddy looked around and saw an older man with a box of poppies standing near the door. Teddy knew he was a war veteran because he wore a military jacket and hat. Veterans were always all over town in the week before Remembrance Day, selling poppies in the mall, in front of banks and grocery stores. . . . But Teddy had never seen one in front of this store before. And he was sure the man hadn't been there when Teddy had entered the store just a few minutes earlier.

Once again, Teddy was caught by surprise. All he could say was, "Excuse me, sir?"

"Do you want a poppy?" the veteran asked. "For Remembrance Day."

"Thank you, sir, but I already have one," Teddy said. "It's under my jacket. We get them at school."

He would have gone on his way then, but the man said,

"Ah, yes, it's good that you wear the poppy you got at school. But I have a special poppy here, and I'd like you to take it."

Teddy suddenly felt uneasy. The man looked friendly enough, but he was a stranger, just like the woman . . . who'd said . . . *Accept the poppy!* Teddy's first thought was that he should run home and tell his parents about the strange people hanging around the convenience store. But the veteran picked a poppy from his box and, smiling like a kindly grandfather, offered it to him.

"This is for you, Teddy Nugent."

Teddy was stunned. *Another* person he'd never met before who knew his name! Were the woman and the veteran some kind of kidnapping team? His legs suddenly seemed paralyzed. If he shouted for help, would Mr. Singh hear him?

"*Accept the poppy*," sounded in Teddy's head. It looked just like the poppy pinned to his shirt and like all the other Remembrance Day poppies he'd seen since he was in kindergarten. A little red paper flower with a black circle in the middle and a pin.

Teddy reached out and accepted the poppy. With his other hand he dug a quarter out of his pocket.

"That's not necessary," the man said. "You can keep your money. There are prices, and there are values."

Teddy gave the veteran a quizzical look and said, "Huh?"

"You *will* pay for it, Teddy, but in another way," said the man. "That is a very special poppy. Keep it close to you tonight. If you find yourself in trouble, say the words to 'In Flanders Fields.' You *do* know them, don't you?"

"Yes," Teddy replied. "But what —"

"Good!" the man interrupted. "But remember, it only works if your situation is desperate. Now, off you go."

It suddenly struck Teddy that there might be something wrong with the veteran. All the oddball things he was saying! Teddy said, "Excuse me, sir, but are you okay?"

The man only replied, "Go home, Teddy."

From behind Teddy came the sudden loud racket of crows caw-cawing. He instinctively turned his head. He saw a flock of the big black birds take off from a tree whose branches bore only scant ragged remains of dead autumn leaves. The crows swept away into the sky and were gone. When Teddy looked back, the veteran was gone, too.

That was just too weird, Teddy kept telling himself as he walked the rest of the way home. The guy must have gone into the store.

Among all the other weirdness was the man asking if he knew the words to "In Flanders Fields." As far as Teddy was concerned, *everybody* knew that famous poem written by Colonel John McCrae, a Canadian army doctor in World War I. Every kid in his class could say it by heart. It was the only poem Teddy had ever had to memorize:

In Flanders fields the poppies blow
Between the crosses, row on row, ...

Teddy stopped at the front door of his house. *Poppies!* Of course! The poem was about poppies in a *graveyard*. Teddy still had the old veteran's poppy in his hand. He held it up close to examine it. He turned it over to see if there was a tiny electronic device stuck on the back. It still looked like any other poppy. Nothing special about it at all! But the man's words, "You will pay . . ." suddenly gave Teddy a creepy feeling.

Teddy didn't tell his parents what had happened at Mr. Singh's store. Parents had a habit of asking a lot of questions if they thought there was something fishy going on. Teddy didn't want to accidentally say anything that might jeopardize his plans for Saturday. But in the middle of supper, Dad dropped a bombshell.

"So, Ted, maybe we'll see you at the arena tomorrow."

Teddy almost choked on a piece of potato. It was a good thing he did, because he immediately thought WHAT! He would have blurted the word out, but the potato got in the way.

His parents both looked alarmed, and Mom asked, "Are you okay, Teddy?"

He nodded that he was and took a drink of milk to wash the potato down. Mom reminded him about chewing his food properly. Those few seconds allowed Teddy to recover from the shock of what his father had said.

War Games strategy!

"Are you guys going to the arena tomorrow?" Teddy asked.

"Of course," Dad replied. "Most years we can't go because November 11 falls on a workday. But this year it falls on a Saturday."

Mom said, "I guess you don't remember when you were little and we all went together on a Sunday."

Teddy might have remembered that if he tried hard enough, but his mind was racing. *My parents are going to be at the arena! Why didn't I think of that? Strategy! Think strategy!*

"You probably won't be able to see me," he said. "There's going to be thousands of kids there, and we all sit in an area that's reserved for schools. The rest of the people sit somewhere else. That's how they do it every year. I probably won't even be able to see you."

"Yeah, you're probably right," said Dad. "But we're not going just to see if we can pick you out of the crowd. We're going for our family members who served in the wars."

"We've shown you their pictures," Mom added. "And their medals, too."

Teddy was anxious to finish supper so he could get to his War Games book. But a thought suddenly struck him and he asked, "Can I see them again?"

"Of course," Dad said, sounding pleased that Teddy was showing interest.

"After you've helped with the dishes," Mom said.

Twenty minutes later, Teddy realized that his parents had misunderstood his request. He'd meant only that he wanted to look at the medals. He wanted to see if any of them were the same as the ones Mr. Sanderson had shown the class. But when he and Dad were seated on the couch in the living room, Mom came in with not only the medals, which were wrapped in purple velvet, but also two thick family photo albums. *Oh no!* he thought. *They're going to show me boring old pictures!*

Teddy looked closely at the medals and said he didn't think they looked like Mr. Sanderson's. His parents asked who Mr. Sanderson was, and Teddy told them he was a Korean War air force veteran who had visited his school.

"There were different medals for different wars, Ted," Dad explained, "and for different branches of the armed forces, too."

He picked one up and said, "This one is called the Military Medal. It was given to your great-great-grandfather, Thomas Nugent, for bravery in the First World War. His brother Joseph was killed in that war, and his name is on the cenotaph in their hometown, in Cape Breton, Nova Scotia."

"Here's the picture of them together," Mom said, pointing to a yellowish photograph of two smiling young men in army uniforms. Teddy had seen the picture before, but only now did he notice the family resemblance to his father. He asked, "Which is the one who died?"

Dad touched the picture and said, "That's Joseph."

"What happened to him?" Teddy asked.

"We don't know exactly," Dad replied. "It was a long time ago. The story passed down in the family is that he was killed in a battle right in front of your great-great-grandfather but that Thomas would never talk about it."

"So Joseph was my great-great-uncle," Teddy said.

"That's right," said Dad. "If Thomas had been killed, too, you and I wouldn't be here today."

Teddy didn't catch on to that at all. What did the distant past have to do with *him*?

Mom flipped a page, pointed to a photo of a young woman and said, "This is my great-aunt Patricia Bidwell. She was a nursing sister."

"Nursing *sister*?" Teddy said. "Is that why she's dressed like a nun?"

"No, no. Not that kind of sister," Mom said. "In those days, nurses were called nursing sisters. Those clothes and that headpiece she's wearing were her uniform. Great Aunt Pat worked in army hospitals in England and France during the First World War. She even met Dr. John McCrae, the man who wrote —"

"In Flanders Fields." Teddy and Dad laughed, because they said it together.

The three of them sat on the couch looking at photographs, images of family members long gone. Grandparents, aunts, uncles and even cousins from succeeding generations. Teddy's parents matched the medals spread out on the purple velvet with the faces in the photographs. A medal called the Atlantic Star had been given to Teddy's great-grandfather, David Steele, for whom Teddy's dad had been named. Commander Steele had been in the navy during World War II and had survived the sinking of his ship by a German U-boat.

Harry Bidwell, a great-grandfather on his mother's side, had been a bomber pilot in the Royal Air Force and had received the Distinguished Flying Cross for carrying out dangerous missions over enemy territory.

After about an hour, Teddy glanced at the digital clock on the cable box. The stuff about the medals and his family members in the wars was cool, and he'd have to tell Paul and Valerie about it. But this family history lesson was taking up time he needed for his War Games book. He didn't want to go to bed too late. War Games competition called for a sharp, wide-awake mind.

Mom finally closed the albums. While she put the books and medals away, Dad said there was a documentary on TV about the Battle of Vimy Ridge.

"Want to watch it with me, Ted?" he asked.

Teddy didn't like documentaries, so he told his dad he had homework. But when he went into his room and closed the door, he felt a bit guilty. He tried to shake off the feeling, telling himself that he *did* have homework; he just wasn't going to do it right now. But the feeling still nagged at him. Then he had an idea!

Besides the Remembrance Day composition, Ms. Potts had given the class a math assignment. Teddy pulled his math textbook and notebook out of his backpack and sat at his desk. The exercise had ten algebra problems. Teddy did one and felt better.

Now, technically, he hadn't deceived his father. He really

hadn't even told his parents any lies concerning the arena. It actually was unlikely that they'd be able to spot him in the crowd — if he was *there*, that is. He'd watch the cable news coverage of the ceremony on the TV in his room, which was almost the same as being there. So he wasn't really being dishonest with *anybody*. Once again, he was very pleased with himself for the way he'd worked things out. He put his math homework away and opened his *War Games Strategy Book*.

For over two hours, Teddy was lost in the world of War Games. He studied the illustrated battle plans in the book and went on his computer to try them out in simulations on the official War Games website. He made notes on his War Games Commander's Field Pad so he could go over them on his way to the mall in the morning. By bedtime, those uncomfortable guilt feelings had long been banished, swept away by Teddy's growing excitement over the competition.

Teddy changed into his pajamas. He was about to crawl into his bed when he noticed the veteran's poppy where he'd left it on his desk. The man had told him to keep it close. Teddy still didn't think there was really anything special about that poppy. But there had been that strange incident with the mirror in the store. And then the older woman. . . .

Teddy thought, *Okay, I'll keep it close, just to prove it's only an ordinary poppy.*

He pinned the poppy to the edge of his pillowcase, with a pencil eraser stuck on the point of the pin so he wouldn't get

pricked while he slept. Then Teddy turned off his lamp, bur-
rowed under the covers, closed his eyes and drifted off. His
last thought was of victory in War Games.

Teddy was soon in a deep sleep. Before his parents went to
bed, his mother opened his door just a crack to peek in on
him and then closed it again. The curtains on Teddy's window were drawn against the chill of a November night but
not all the way. A shaft of moonlight found its way through
the narrow opening. It crept across the darkness of Teddy's
room and fell upon the poppy pinned to the pillowcase just
a hand's breadth from Teddy's head. The poppy glowed scar-
let in the silver light.

2
The Dugout
and No Man's Land

WHUMP! THE NOISE JARRED Teddy awake. His bed shook. Just as he opened his eyes and mouth, something gritty poured down on his face, blinding and choking him. His brain flashed *Earthquake! Mom and Dad!*

Panicking, Teddy sat bolt upright — and hit his head on something where there should have been nothing. He fell back, stunned, and gagging on whatever was in his mouth. He half-turned to spit it out. With one hand, he tried to clear the grit from his eyes. His other hand groped for his bedside lamp but couldn't find it.

Must have fallen over, he thought. *This is weird! We don't get earthquakes here!*

There was another, even louder WHUMP, and it seemed like the whole room shook. Teddy felt more stuff fall on him. It was like someone was throwing sand on him at the beach. He spat out a gob of something and tried to shout "*Mom!*" But it came out as a feeble croak.

A voice said, "Looks like buddy there is awake."

Another voice responded, "Them Jack Johnsons'll do it. Might as well roll out of the sack, b'y. Your ma's not here with your mornin' tea."

Bad dream! Teddy thought. *Just need to dream something else.*

Then a hand was on his shoulder and a wet cloth wiped his face. *Mom?*

Someone said, "Let's get the muck out of your eyes, skipper, so you can meet your dugout buddies."

Dugout buddies? That's not Mom! Come on, Teddy! You're dreaming that you're dreaming. Wake up so you can go back to sleep.

He felt the cloth dab at his eyes. *Not real!*

Then he could open his eyes again. From beneath an old-fashioned army helmet, a face was looking down at him. It was in shadow, so he couldn't make out the features. *Still dreaming! Wake up, Teddy, wake up!*

Teddy blinked and looked past the soldier crouched beside his bed. Then he realized that he wasn't in his own bed. He wasn't even in his room. He was in some kind of a *cave.* He said, "Where . . ." But his mouth was still gummed up.

The soldier turned and said, "Hand me a cup of water, Joe. He's still chewin' on the interior décor."

"Comin' right up, Tom," said someone behind the soldier. "Room service with a smile. Don't forget the tip."

A moment later, Teddy sipped water from a tin cup and swished it in his mouth. He still told himself, *A dream, a dream, a dream!* But he was less and less convinced each time he thought it.

"Don't swallow it, buddy," Tom said, "unless you like mud."

"Main course on the menu around here," said Joe.

"Ahh, b'y, don't be so discouragin.' I think buddy here is pretty green," said Tom. "Folded up his uniform nice and regulation neat and went to bed in his long johns."

He said to Teddy, "First time in the trenches, right, buddy?"

Teddy wanted to go to the bathroom to get rid of the bad-tasting slop in his mouth. *But where's the bathroom?* He remembered the time he dreamed that he got up to go to the bathroom to pee and then woke up to find he'd peed in his bed. He didn't want anything like *that* happening again. But could people *spit* in their sleep?

Joe must have noticed Teddy's bulging cheeks. He said, "Spit 'er on the floor, b'y. We got maid service."

Teddy spurted a stream, caught his breath and gasped, "Trenches?"

"Get up and get dressed, buddy," Tom said. "And this time, mind your head."

Teddy realized that he was indeed wearing old-fashioned

long johns and not his pajamas. On a trunk beside his cot lay a neatly folded brown army uniform — pants, shirt and tunic — covered with dirt. His bed was just a rough bunk in a recess dug into an earth wall. There was so little headroom, he couldn't sit upright. Not until he got out of the bunk and stepped away from it could he stand up straight — in his underwear.

"Better take care of them long johns, buddy," Joe said. "The ones the army gives us are just like an epidemic. They go through the ranks."

Tom laughed, but the joke was lost on Teddy. He wasn't even paying attention. As he dressed himself, he finally got a good look at the room in which he'd awakened — if he really was awake.

Low light glowed from a lantern sitting on top of a barrel, throwing shadows across the room. Teddy saw two other bunk-niches in the earthen walls, and trunks identical to his beside them. The low ceiling, also of earth, was supported by a few wooden beams that didn't look very safe to him. The floor was made of unevenly spaced boards. Mud oozed up between them. The only doorway Teddy could see was an opening covered by a tarpaulin hanging on the outside, like the flap on a camping tent.

In the middle of the room was a small crate that served as a table. On it was the thick white stub of an unlit candle, a deck of playing cards and a big tin can with a lid on it from which Joe had poured the cup of water. Three stools were the only other items that could pass for furniture. The rest of the room's contents were a jumble of things that made it look like a cluttered basement. Many of them were strange to Teddy, like the metal box that seemed to be some kind of heater. A pipe stretched from its back up through the ceiling. Slumped against the wall was an open, coarse sack, half-filled with potatoes. A wooden box beside it held a few carrots, onions and turnips. Scattered about the room were shovels, picks and buckets — one of which was filled with pieces of jagged metal. From pegs in the beams hung water canteens, knapsacks, knitted caps and leather pouches with buckles on them that made Teddy think of Batman's utility belt. He might have wondered what was in them, but something else in the room seized his attention. Guns!

Three rifles, leaning upright against each other like a tripod, stood near the entrance. Their butts were on the floor and their barrels pointed upward. Unlike everything else in the room, there was nothing untidy about the guns. They looked like they were exactly where they were supposed to be, and the metal parts gleamed as though they had just been cleaned.

A rat suddenly dashed across the floor and disappeared under a cot. Teddy would have jumped out of his socks, but he hadn't pulled them on yet.

"Don't worry about the boarders," Joe said. "You'll get used to them."

"But not the lice," said Tom, scratching at his underarm. "You never get used to the lice."

"Lice?" Teddy said. "I don't have lice."

Tom chuckled and said, "Buddy, if you weren't lousy when you got here last night, you probably are by now. Joe and I don't share them on purpose. They just jump onto fresh meat as soon as it gets here."

Teddy remembered Dad saying something about pinching yourself to wake up from a dream. That was his way out of their weirdness! He picked a spot on his arm and pinched himself so hard that he let out an "Ouch!" It didn't work. He was still in the cave.

"Found one already?" Joe laughed.

Now the realization crept into Teddy's mind that he wasn't dreaming. That something very weird indeed was happening to him. He recalled what the old veteran had said: "If you find yourself in trouble, say the words to 'In Flanders Fields.'"

Right away, Teddy began to recite the familiar line: "In Flanders fields the poppies blow."

Nothing happened. Then he remembered that the old man had also said, "It only works if your situation is desperate."

Teddy thought, *I'm in a cave with rats and lice. It's kind of smelly in here, too. How bad does it have to be to be desperate?*

"Well, b'y, let's hear the rest of it," said Tom.

Teddy saw that Tom and Joe were looking at him and glancing at each other as though they thought something was funny. He just said, "What?"

"You were saying Colonel McCrae's poem," said Joe. "I won't ask why in the world you'd suddenly bust out saying a poem, but if a man wants to say a poem, he's got every right to do it. So give us the rest of it. We love poetry, don't we, Tom?"

"I say a line of Shakespeare myself first thing every morning when I wake up," Tom replied. "To pee or not to pee."

Teddy could tell they were joking with him, but he was too confused to find anything funny. He would have felt silly reciting the poem. It also struck him as weird that Joe had referred to him as a *man*. Couldn't these guys see that he was a kid?"

"I don't know the rest of it," Teddy lied. "You said I got here last night. What time was that?"

"Don't *you* know?" Joe asked.

Before Teddy could reply, another WHUMP shook the room and dirt fell from the ceiling.

"What *is* that?" Teddy cried.

"Just another Jack Johnson," Joe said. "Fritz ought to be more careful with those things. He might hurt somebody. Say, you aren't already shell-shocked, are you?"

Teddy didn't know what Joe was talking about. Tom said, "Naa, Joe. I told you, he's just green." Then he asked Teddy, "What's your name, bud?"

"Teddy Nugent."

"*Nugent!*" Tom exclaimed. "That's our name. I'm Tom Nugent, and this is my brother, Joe. You can probably already tell that he's the fool in the family."

"Right you are," said Joe. "I enlisted first. But then Tom was fool enough to follow me."

"Where are you from, Ted?" Tom asked.

Teddy told him. Tom said, "Must be a different bunch of Nugents. Joe and I are from Cape Breton. You know, the island that's the best part of Nova Scotia."

Teddy's response was little more than a whisper. "I've heard of it."

The names flashed in his mind. *Thomas and Joseph Nugent — from Cape Breton!* His great-great-grandfather and his great-great-uncle! He'd seen their photograph in the family album. But . . . the faces of these men in the cave didn't look quite the same as the ones in the picture. In the photograph, Thomas and Joseph were smiling. Their faces were clean-shaven and beaming with good health.

The Tom and Joe that Teddy was looking at now had whisker stubble. There were more lines in their faces — the sort his mother called worry lines. Their eyes had a weary look, and their faces made Teddy think of people who had lost weight because of illness.

But how could this be? If he wasn't dreaming, how could he possibly be here with them? Thomas Nugent had died of old age years before Teddy was born. And Joseph . . . Teddy could hear his father's words: "*He was killed in a battle right in front of your great-great-grandfather.*"

The thought struck Teddy like a blast of cold water. *Joe is going to be killed!* He wanted to say something, but he didn't know what. Then he realized that Tom was talking to him.

"Joe and I were on a two-day leave," he said. "You know, a

little break from the war to enjoy the beauty and hospitality of France."

France? Teddy thought. *I'm in France?*

"Beautiful country," Joe said. "If you like mud, France is the place for you. I just might take a bottle of it home to remind me of this wonderful trip when I'm an old grandfather."

"Ahh, b'y, there you go again," said Tom. "Teddy, don't you pay any attention to old misery there. We have some good times when we get out of these trenches. There's good food and wine in the cafés, and if you go to the farmhouses, the women will cook you up a plate of the tastiest lunch you ever had. They call it *pommes frites*. But us Canucks call it French fried potatoes. Put a little salt and vinegar on it, or maybe a bit of mustard, and it's delicious."

"But don't let 'em rob you," Joe warned. "They see that Canadian uniform, and they'll make you pay twice as much as they charge the British Tommies. These French people think us Canucks are made of money."

Tom said, "Joe, I'll send your complaints to King George."

"That's good, buddy," Joe replied. "Tell me when you get an answer. I'll add it to our letters from Prime Minister Borden, President Wilson and the Kaiser."

"Didn't I tell you he's the family fool?" Tom said. "But like I was telling you, Ted, we were on leave. When we got back last night, you were already asleep. We didn't wake you. We just figured you were the replacement for the last man who slept in that bunk."

"What happened to him?" Teddy asked.

"He went to church," Joe replied. "Five days ago."

Teddy said, "You mean, he went to church and didn't come back?"

Joe chuckled, but there was no mirth in it. "No, Ted, old buddy. I mean he's dead."

Tom explained. "When a soldier gets killed, we say he went to church. We got our own lingo in the trenches. You'll pick it up."

"A Jack Johnson got poor old Charlie," Joe said. "We only knew him for a few weeks, but he was a pretty good fella. About your age, Ted. How old are you? Twenty?"

Teddy thought, *this is too weird. I don't look like I'm twenty. Or do I . . . to them?*

"Yes," he replied. "I'm . . . twenty. What's a Jack Johnson?"

"A Hun artillery shell," Tom said. "We named them after the heavyweight boxing champion because they have a big punch. One exploded just a few feet from poor Charlie, and the shrapnel got him."

"Shrapnel?" Teddy said.

"B'y, didn't they teach you anything?" Joe asked. He went to the bucket Teddy had noticed earlier and took out a piece of jagged metal. It was about the size of Teddy's hand, and thin, with sharp edges.

"Shrapnel kills more soldiers than bullets, gas or anything else," Joe said. "Some of it is steel balls the size of marbles that are packed into the shells. When the shell explodes, they fly out like a shotgun blast. Pieces of the shell casing, like this one, whiz through the air like red hot razors. Slice through a man like your dad's knife carving up the Christmas turkey."

Teddy stared at the object in Joe's hand. It looked like a piece of junk. But the thought of those sharp, mean-looking edges cutting into his flesh sent a chill through him. He asked, "Why do you have a bucket full of that stuff?"

"Souvenirs," Tom said. "When the war is over and we go home, we're going to take souvenirs, just like people do when they've been to Niagara Falls."

Joe interrupted. "You ever seen Niagara Falls, Ted?"

"Yes, I have," Teddy replied. "Lots of times."

Joe said, "Prove it."

"Well, I can't *prove* it," Teddy said. "But I've been there. Honest."

"That's why we keep these souvenirs," Tom said. "Proof, for all the war stories we'll tell the people at home."

Then Joe said, "This bucket of shrapnel is also our own little trophy collection."

"Enough of that now, Joe," Tom said. He nudged Teddy and said, "He goes on like this every time a new man comes into the dugout. Ignore it."

Joe continued as though Tom hadn't spoken. "All the pieces of shrapnel in this bucket were supposed to kill us, but didn't. So far, between me and Tom and the Huns, me and Tom are winning. So those are our war trophies. Nobody has pinned any medals on us, but we have these. Every other man that bunked with us has gone to church, but Fritz can't kill the Nugent brothers. Right, Tom?"

Teddy was alarmed to hear that all of his predecessors had been killed. Fear must have shown in his face because Tom said, "Cut it out, Joe. You're scarier than the Jack Johnsons. Pay him no mind, Teddy. Just do like we do, and you'll be okay."

"Of course you'll be okay," Joe said. "You're in luck, Ted, because your name is Nugent. It doesn't matter that you're not from Cape Breton. As far as Tom and I are concerned, you're family, and that means Fritz can't kill you."

It was all happening faster than Teddy's brain could process. He knew that Joe would never go home. He knew that Tom would be awarded a medal. Most bewildering of all, he knew that he *was* their family . . . just a couple of "greats" removed. The thought struck him that if he ever tried to explain this unbelievable story to his friends, Paul would make a joke like, "So did you hit your great-great grandpa for a couple of bucks?" And Valerie would roll her eyes and let out a huff.

For a moment, Teddy thought he actually heard the sound. But the cover of the entrance to the dugout was suddenly opened with a loud flapping noise, followed by a gust of cold air. Tom and Joe snapped to attention as a soldier stepped in. Teddy quickly guessed from the man's uniform and Tom and Joe's reaction that he was an officer, so he stood to attention, too.

The man took a quick look around the room and said, "Anyone care to tell me why you men aren't outside for morning parade?"

"Very sorry, Captain," Tom said. "A couple of those shells Fritz sent over shook things up in here."

"That's no excuse, Private Nugent," the captain barked. "You think you're the only groundhogs whose burrow took a dusting? Some of the boys got buried. But they still crawled out of their holes for parade. What were you waiting for, an INVITATION?"

He shouted the last word.

"No, sir," Tom said, "We . . ."

"It's my fault, Captain," Teddy said. "I'm the new kid. . . . I mean, I'm the replacement. I just arrived last night, and these men have been . . . well . . . they weren't outside because I was asleep and they saved me from choking on dirt after the Jack Johnsons hit. If it weren't for them, I'd be in church by now."

"Is that so?" the captain said. "How commendable of them." Something about his tone told Teddy that the captain wasn't buying his story. Ms. Potts sounded like that when she knew a kid was making up an excuse for not having homework done.

"What's your name, soldier?" the captain asked.

When Teddy told him, the captain said, "Nugent? Don't tell me I have another Nugent brother in my command."

"No, sir," Teddy said. "We're . . . not related."

"But we'll look after him like he's family, sir," Joe said.

"Then make sure he puts his helmet on during a bombardment," the captain said. "And the next time I see him, he'd better be wearing his puttees and boots."

Teddy was standing in his socks. He realized that he was supposed to know what puttees were, so he didn't ask. He guessed they were the khaki-coloured wrappings that Joe and Tom had around their legs below the knees.

The captain told the three Nugents to get themselves outside for parade and then left. Tom let out a breath of relief. Joe thumped Teddy on the shoulder. "That was real jake of you, Ted, speaking up like that."

"Jake?" said Teddy. "Is that a nickname?"

"It means *good*," Tom said. "Now finish getting dressed so we can go out and hear the birdies sing."

"Birdies?" said Teddy. "Like larks?"

"More like vultures," Joe replied.

Teddy sat on his cot to put his boots on. In each of them he found a rolled-up puttee. When he started to clumsily wrap one around his leg, Joe said, "B'y, they didn't teach you anything, did they? Let me show you."

As Joe demonstrated how to wind a puttee around his leg, Teddy asked, "What are these things for?"

"Well, Teddy me boy," Joe replied, "some officer might tell you that they give your legs support on a long march. But as far as I'm concerned, they're a damned nuisance that don't do nothin' at all. Some fool of a general decided that he liked the look of them, and that's why we're stuck with them."

A few minutes later, after a quick trip to a smelly latrine, Teddy stood outside in front of the dugout with Joe and Tom. He was in a trench. He'd stepped from one strange place in which he was part of a scene where he didn't belong, into another. He wore a steel helmet that felt cold on his head, poorly fitting boots, and the puttees that Joe had wrapped too tightly. Attached to his belt were a pouch for ammunition and another for a first-aid kit, a bag that contained a gas mask and a sheath that held a long, sharply pointed bayonet. The rifle he held in his hands was heavier than it looked. He thought of the video games he'd played that had combat soldiers brandishing big guns as though they were lighter than air.

Teddy didn't hear any "birdies" singing. From not far away came a rumbling noise that he now knew was the sound of artillery fire. The air was cold, and drizzle fell from an overcast sky. Water dripped from the rim of his helmet. Teddy was thankful for the big coat — Tom had called it a greatcoat — that he wore. But he had a queasy feeling that it had once belonged to the unfortunate Charlie.

To Teddy's left and right, other soldiers stood in front of dugout entrances while the captain inspected their rifles and equipment. This was "parade." Teddy couldn't see far down the line either way, because the trench hadn't been dug in a straight line. It was only a few feet wide — just enough room for soldiers going in opposite directions to pass each other. The walls were shored up with sandbags piled almost seven feet high. A floor of boards kept Teddy's feet out of the mud, but the steady drizzle had made the bottom of the trench swampy, so he stood in water almost up to his ankles. He soon discovered that his uncomfortable boots also leaked. Under his clothing, in his armpits and other places, Teddy felt itchy. Tom had been right about the lice.

Teddy had thought the dugout was smelly, but out here the air was heavy with an odour that almost made him gag. It was sickly, worse than the smell of the latrine. It reminded him of the time he and Paul had filled a jar with dew worms for fishing and then forgot about it. When they finally took the lid off the jar, the stench of rotting dead worms almost knocked them off their feet. Paul joked about it later. Teddy couldn't think of anything funny about this inescapable, foul smell.

Tom had told him that no talking was allowed during parade. But as Teddy drew the sour air in with every breath, he couldn't help whispering, "What stinks?"

Tom whispered back, "No man's land."

The captain bellowed, "QUIET ON PARADE!"

After a breakfast of canned meat called bully beef, stale biscuits and tea without milk or sugar, Teddy, Joe and Tom were put to work. They had to help other soldiers repair damage that artillery shells had done to the sandbag emplacements. It was hard labour that involved a lot of shovelling and hauling sacks of sand made even heavier by the rain. Teddy discovered that the trench zigzagged to minimize the effects of exploding shells. He learned that the trench he was in was the front line of a vast maze of connected trenches that stretched for many miles. It was like a giant community all its own, populated by thousands of soldiers. But it was a community no one would live in if they didn't have to.

He asked Joe, "What if one of those Jack Johnsons lands here?"

"We'd get blown up," Joe replied, as casually as if he were answering a question about the weather. "But this isn't a *real* bombardment. Just Fritz saying good morning. Our gunners are polite and send the same greeting back. When the Huns decide to come across no man's land for personal introductions, you'll know what a real bombardment is, because it's like a hell you never heard about in Sunday school. But don't you worry, buddy. You're protected by the Nugent luck."

Teddy didn't feel reassured. Every so often, he heard the crack of a rifle shot. Sometimes it sounded far away. Other times it came from very close by. A shot might be followed by several more in quick succession, like the sounds of a gunfight in a movie. Or there might be a single shot and then nothing for a while.

"Snipers," Tom said. "The Huns try to kill ours, and we try to kill theirs."

"They pick off anybody foolish enough to poke their heads up," Joe added. "So you keep your pumpkin down, Ted. Otherwise, some Fritzie with a sharp eye will draw bead on you, and your mother will get a sad telegram."

Teddy thought the whole situation was bizarre, crazy, *insane*! He was in a horrible, foul-smelling world where people were actually killing each other — where people actually wanted to kill *him*. Fritz, the Huns — whatever other names Tom and Joe had for the Germans — would shoot at him with real bullets if he so much as showed his head. If Teddy lost in a War Games competition, he got up from the table and went home. But here . . .

An explosion suddenly shattered the air with a thunderous blast that hit Teddy's ears like a hammer blow and left them ringing. The ground shook, and the muddy water at the bottom of the trench seethed. Nearby, a plume of smoke and dirt shot up like a geyser. Joe, Tom and the other soldiers in the work crew dropped whatever was in their hands and flattened themselves against the sandbag walls. Teddy stood petrified with fear and confusion. Joe jumped up and hauled him down. "Didn't they teach you anything?" he growled, as Teddy's head smacked against burlap.

A horde of rats surged by, leaping and swimming in a frantic attempt to escape destruction. One squealing rodent climbed onto Teddy's leg. He cried out, and Joe knocked it away with a swipe of his hand. "No pets," he said. "Regulations."

Smoke drifted into the trench from around a corner. Teddy thought the acrid smell was like that of the Canada Day fireworks he watched every year with his parents but multiplied by a hundred. It made his eyes water, and it burned in his nose and mouth.

A sergeant lurched out of the smoke, his face black with grime. He was coughing and spitting. Teddy gasped when he saw a shard of metal like one of Joe's "trophies" sticking out of his thigh.

"You men, get over here now," the sergeant croaked. "There's casualties."

Teddy, Joe, Tom and the others hurried around the corner to a scene of horror. An artillery shell had fallen directly into the trench. The explosion had wreaked devastation. Sand spilled out of shredded bags. Red-stained water ran into a big crater in the bottom of the trench. Splintered wood lay everywhere. But it was the sight of the casualties that numbed Teddy's senses.

All along the section of trench, from where Teddy stood to the next corner, lay torn and bloody forms of men. Some of them were as lifeless as the sandbags. *Gone to church* flashed through Teddy's mind. Others writhed and kicked and even tried to stand up but couldn't. The wounded men shouted curses, moaned in pain and cried. Teddy couldn't stand to look anymore or to hear anymore. Under his breath, he started to say, "In Flanders fields . . ."

"Come on, Ted," said Tom, pushing a shovel into his hands. "Some of the lads were buried. We have to work fast."

Teddy immediately forgot about his own situation. Someone else's was more desperate. Soldiers had been trapped under piles of dirt and debris when their dugouts caved in. Some would be injured, and all were in danger of suffocation. Teddy went to work with the shovel, joining Tom, Joe and a growing team of diggers to save them. As the rescuers pulled men out of holes that might have been their graves, stretcher-bearers cleared the trench of the human carnage. They carried away the dead, the wounded and the severed body parts of both. Every moment that Teddy worked and watched what was going on around him, his mind was filled with the morbid wonder that in the next instant, he, too, might be blown to bits.

After all the survivors had been found and the last corpses recovered, Teddy and his companions were allowed to stop for a rest. They sipped a lukewarm, salty drink Tom called beef bouillon from tin cups. Teddy didn't like it, but it was better than nothing. He sat there in fear and misery, sickened by the nearness of so much death. He huddled in wet clothes that provided little comfort from the chill air and the constant drizzle. He was exhausted. He'd seen terrible things he'd never wanted to see and wished never to see again. But even as Teddy wondered why people should be put in such an awful situation, the thought came to him that everything he'd seen had been within the narrow confines of the trench.

"What's it like . . . out there?" he asked Tom.

"Out there? You mean no man's land?" Tom said. "B'y, you don't want to know."

"Like a walk in the park," Joe said. "Take along a picnic basket and stop for lunch by a scenic shell hole. There's thousands to choose from. The shooting is good, too, if you're a sportsman."

"Ahh, there goes my foolish brother again," Tom said. "Joe, did I ever tell you that when you were a baby, Da and Mama used to play catch with you, and they dropped you on your head?"

"That's why I started wearing a helmet," Joe replied. "Been wearing one ever since."

"I want to see no man's land," Teddy said. He didn't know why he'd blurted those words out. What he'd seen in the trench was ugly enough. Then the thought came to him. *Maybe out there, the most crucial part of this real war game was played, and he just had to see it.*

"Poke your head up, buddy, and it'll be the last thing you see," said Joe.

"Joe is right," said Tom. "But there is a way you can take a look. Just wait here a moment."

Tom hurried off down the trench and around a corner. When he was gone, Joe said, "Tom lied. Da and Mama didn't drop me on my head. They dropped me on my bum, and I bounced."

Teddy laughed, much to his own surprise. Soon Tom returned carrying an odd-looking oblong box. "I borrowed this from an artillery spotter," he said. "It's a periscope, Ted."

Teddy had seen submarine periscopes in movies. The thing Tom had didn't look anything like them. It was a rectangular, wooden green box about two feet long and five inches wide. There was a small glass window on one side at the top and another on the opposite side at the bottom. Tom said, "It has mirrors inside, so you can look over the edge of the trench without exposing yourself."

"The trick is to not look too long," said Joe. "If Fritz spots it, he'll put a bullet into it."

"Joe is right again," Tom said. "You take a look, then you pull it down and move to another spot, first this way, then that way. Keeps Fritzie guessing. And here's another trick."

Tom scooped up a handful of mud and smeared it over the upper half of the periscope, covering everything but the glass. "Makes it harder for Fritz to see it," he said. Then he pulled a pair of binoculars from his coat pocket.

"The spotter loaned me these, too. You can use them to look through the periscope. That will protect your eyes in case a Hun gets off a lucky shot."

"Give you a good close look at the enemy, too," Joe said. "You might see Fritz give you a big smile before he tries for that lucky shot."

Joe told Teddy to get on the fire step, the narrow ledge the soldiers stood on so they could fire their rifles if the Germans attacked, but to keep his head down. Tom held the periscope while Teddy looked through it with the binoculars. Every thirty seconds or so, Joe said, "Move," and Teddy shifted from one spot to another. No bullets smashed into the periscope, so Teddy got a look at something he'd never forget.

He was stunned to see the foremost German trenches so close to him. Couldn't the enemy just attack at any time? Whoever the generals were, they knew nothing of the kind of tactics and strategies he'd studied in the War Games book. But nothing Teddy had ever experienced anywhere compared to the desolation that was no man's land.

Between the coils of barbed wire that stretched in silent menace along both the German and Allied lines lay a nightmarish landscape. Repeated pounding by artillery had churned the soggy ground into a mass of mud, cratered with big shell holes. Here and there stood the charred, skeletal remains of what had once been trees, looking like they belonged in a ghost movie. But this wasn't a movie.

The ground was littered with the debris of battle: rifles, helmets, knapsacks, broken stretchers. And bodies. And pieces of bodies. Human remains lay in the mud like so much cast-off garbage. Corpses were bloated and barely recognizable as men. Teddy noticed flurries of movement and then realized that crows were scavenging, just like he'd seen them do when an animal had been killed on a highway.

Teddy had seen enough of no man's land. He handed the binoculars to Joe, got down from the fire step and sat on a sandbag. He felt sick to his stomach.

"So many bodies out there," he said. "Are they our men?"

"Some of them," Tom replied. "Some are Huns. Some are British and French. Us Canucks aren't the first ones in these trenches. Sometimes our side attacks the Huns. Sometimes they attack us. Men get killed out there. Lots of men."

"Then there's the night raids," Joe said. "Our boys and the Fritzies take turns sneaking across no man's land to pay each other friendly visits. Not everybody makes it back to their own lines."

"Couldn't somebody go out and get the dead men?" Teddy asked. "Shouldn't they be given a proper burial?"

"Every so often there's a truce," Tom said. "We pick up our dead and wounded, and the Huns pick up theirs. But with men being buried in mud and falling into shell holes, you never find them all."

"Then the artillery barrages rearrange the real estate again," Joe said. "Your buddy who got killed one week disappears into the ground, and what's left of him pops up the next week."

Tom said, "The ground out there is soaked with blood and death. That's why no man's land stinks like rotten meat."

Tom had to return the periscope and binoculars to the artillery spotter. While he was gone, Teddy said to Joe, "When I looked at the German trench, I saw a big long hill behind it."

He stopped himself from saying that on a War Games competition table, something like that would be considered a strategic objective worth capturing.

"That's not actually a hill," said Joe. "It's called Vimy Ridge."

Vimy Ridge! Teddy recognized that name. Canadian soldiers had fought a famous battle there. Before he went to bed, his dad had wanted him to watch a documentary about it. Teddy leaned back against the parapet and closed his eyes. He wished he'd stayed up and watched that program with his dad. Maybe he wouldn't be here now. He was very tired. Even though he was cold and wet, he dozed off.

Teddy had one of those dreams in which a person seems to be dreaming that they're dreaming. People floated in and out. Paul was there, telling him to make sure he was wearing his puttees so he'd be properly dressed for the War Games competition. Valerie rolled her eyes at him and huffed. Ms. Potts said she'd know if he cheated on his Remembrance Day composition. The older woman from Mr. Singh's store told him she'd see him soon. The veteran who'd given him the poppy smiled at him like a kindly grandfather but didn't say a word.

Then Joe was there. But he was like a phantom, fading as he said, "You're family, b'y. I'm glad I had the chance to meet you, Teddy."

"Teddy. *Ted!* Wake up."

A man's voice broke into Teddy's dream. His consciousness was momentarily suspended in that foggy state between dream and wakefulness. Teddy thought he was finally back in his own bed. He murmured, "Dad?"

A hand grasped his arm and shook it. Suddenly wide awake, Teddy opened his eyes. Tom was crouched beside him.

"No, b'y, I'm not your da, and I'm not your mama either. Wakey-wakey, buddy. We're moving out of here in a few minutes."

Teddy looked around in bewilderment. He wasn't in his own bed. He wasn't sitting on a sandbag in the trench. He was sitting on the ground with his back against the wall in some sort of cave. The dugout? No. It was somewhere else. Not a cave. More like an underground passageway. Old-fashioned light bulbs hung from electrical wires strung along the low ceiling. The glaring light revealed a narrow corridor with rough, chalky white walls. It was full of soldiers who were putting on helmets, sliding their arms through the straps of backpacks and fixing bayonets onto the ends of their rifles. The stuffy air smelled of sweat and urine. From somewhere came a muted rumbling noise. Teddy felt tremors in the ground, and white dust like baby powder fell from the ceiling.

Confused, Teddy said, "Where am I?" The question was more to himself than for Tom.

Tom said, "Come on, Ted, shake yourself. We're in the tunnels."

"Tunnels?" Teddy said.

"Don't I wish I could do that?"

It was Joe, who Teddy thought had just spoken to him in his dream, but now stood next to Tom.

"Do what?" Teddy asked.

"Fall asleep for an hour and forget the past two days," Joe said. "Ted, old buddy, I'm going to try that when I get home. Sleep for as long as it takes to forget the whole blasted war."

Teddy thought, *two days? A few minutes ago, I was . . .*

"This is it, lads! Move forward! Keep it orderly."

The captain that Teddy had met in the dugout stood a short distance from him, barking orders and encouragement to the soldiers trudging past him.

"You men don't like it down here? Think how surprised

the Huns will be when you come up right in their faces. We're taking Vimy Ridge, boys! For king and country!"

Teddy had no time to wonder at the madness of it all. Tom pulled him to his feet, and Joe thrust his rifle into his hands. Then they were caught up in the press of soldiers surging forward.

One moment, Teddy was carried along in a human torrent rushing through the tunnel. Then he was outside in the chill darkness of pre-dawn. He emerged into a maelstrom that was chaotic, disorienting, terrifying. A stiff wind pummelled his back with sleet. Flares rocketed up from the German lines. Tracer shells streaked overhead. The thunder of artillery pounded in his ears mercilessly. Shells exploded with air-shattering bursts of fire — so many of them that it seemed as if all the stars were being blasted out of the sky. Fountains of mud erupted all around him.

On the other side of no man's land, a rain of artillery shells obliterated the foremost German trenches in an explosive inferno. Then the torrent of destruction crept further into enemy territory. Like a living thing, it walked up the slope, seeking to annihilate everything in its path.

Like all the other soldiers rushing toward the looming form of Vimy Ridge, Teddy dodged around gaping craters. Tom and Joe were a little way ahead of him, and he was determined to stay close to them. Teddy saw pulsing flashes of fire along the line of the German trench and on the lower level of the ridge. The *boom-boom* of explosions was punctuated by the staccato racket of enemy machine guns. The artillery hadn't knocked all of them out. Teddy was sure he could hear bullets buzz past his head like angry hornets. He saw men throw their arms up protectively in front of their faces, just as they would in a howling Canadian snowstorm. But this was a blizzard of bullets. Many soldiers dropped, stopped in their tracks as suddenly as if they had run into an invisible wall. One was Joe.

Teddy had almost caught up to Joe when right in front of him, Joe doubled over as though he'd been punched in the stomach. He dropped his rifle, staggered a few steps and then fell in the mud. Tom didn't see his brother go down and kept running toward the enemy lines.

Teddy cried out, "Joe! Tom! Tom, Joe's hurt. *TOM*!"

His cries were lost in the din of the battlefield, and Tom didn't hear him.

Teddy ran to where Joe lay face down in the muck. He dropped his rifle, knelt down and turned him over. Joe's face was smeared with mud, but his eyes were wide open. He coughed and blood frothed from his mouth. Joe whispered, "Nugent luck."

Teddy wasn't even sure if Joe was still alive when a sergeant grabbed him by the back of the neck and hauled him to his feet.

"Pick up that rifle, soldier, and advance!"

Teddy's eyes welled with tears. "But this is Joe," he protested. "He's my . . ."

"Best friend, brother, cousin, uncle!" the sergeant said.

"You can't help him, laddie. The stretcher bearers will pick him up. Your duty is to advance."

Teddy had known that Joe would be killed. But he'd never imagined it would happen right in front of him, never thought that it would hit him like the loss of a loved one he'd known all his life. Gripped by fear and grief, Teddy was on the verge of saying, "In Flanders fields . . ."

But he couldn't abandon Tom. He remembered what his father had said about the family story — that Tom had seen Joe killed but wouldn't talk about it. Teddy knew that Joe had gone to church. He had to catch up to Tom and tell him.

Teddy picked up his rifle, and with a shove from the sergeant, pushed on toward enemy lines. Tom was somewhere ahead of him in that mass of soldiers advancing on Vimy Ridge under a sky aflame, and he had to find him. Teddy had gone but a few steps when a shell hit the ground very close to him and exploded in a blinding flash. Heat seared his face. The blast lifted Teddy right off his feet and flung him backwards. He landed in the mud, dazed and numbed. For a moment, the numbness gave way to pain. Then he slipped out of consciousness into a merciful oblivion.

Teddy dreamed of seeing Joe killed. He saw Tom searching for his brother on the smoking battlefield and then weeping at Joe's grave. It was one of thousands marked by plain wooden crosses.

Between the crosses, row on row

He saw Joe's name on the cenotaph in his hometown, in

Cape Breton, Nova Scotia. Then Teddy was standing in front of the cenotaph in his own community, a monument he'd passed by hundreds — no, *thousands* — of times. He stared in disbelief at his own name engraved on a bronze plaque that was tinted green with age.

Teddy's mind rebelled at that vision. *No! It's wrong. I'm not dead. I'M NOT DEAD!*

"No, love, you're not dead."

It was a woman's voice. Teddy had another fleeting moment in which he thought he was back in his own bed. He realized he actually was in bed. He said, "Mom?"

Teddy tried to open his eyes, but something was very wrong. It wasn't just that his eyelids wouldn't open, like on mornings when they were crusted with what Paul grossly called eye-snot. It was more like his eyes didn't work at all.

"I'm not your mum, love," the woman said. "Now, you've got to lie quiet. The doctor will be here to talk to you as soon as he can. He'll be very pleased indeed that you're awake. You've been with us for three days."

She had an English accent. Teddy thought he'd heard her voice before, but he didn't try to remember where. He was starting to feel panicky. Why couldn't he see anything? He tried to raise his arms, only to find them snugly confined under a blanket. He struggled to free them, but the effort drained his strength.

"Now, now, love. No need for that. Here's a nice drink of water. You must be thirsty after such a long sleep."

Teddy felt the touch of a cup on his lips. His anxiety subsided a little as he sipped, and then gulped the cool water.

"Not so much at once, Ted," the woman said, taking the cup away from his mouth. "You'll choke."

Teddy coughed out a mouthful of water, gasped, and said, "You know my name?"

The woman said, "Oh yes, I know you, Teddy Nugent."

The woman in Mr. Singh's store! But could she ... He knew how, without really knowing. It was the work of whatever weird power had snatched him from his own bed in his own room. The woman kept talking in her calm, gentle tone.

"Did you think the ambulance men would just leave you at the hospital without telling us who you are?"

Hospital?

"Mind you, love, you did a lot of talking in your sleep. All about your mates, Joe and Tom."

"Tom!" Teddy cried suddenly. Once more he fought to get out from under the blanket, and again he sagged back on the bed, immediately exhausted.

"Quiet, Teddy," the woman said, placing a hand on his head. "You must stay quiet."

"But I have to find Tom," Teddy said frantically. "He didn't really see Joe killed. That's why he never talked about it. He kept advancing on Vimy Ridge, and Joe was killed behind him, and then Tom looked for him and found his grave ... and ... *Why can't I see you?*"

A man's voice came into Teddy's darkness.

"Nurse, the orderly told me Private Nugent is awake. Well, are you back with us, young man?"

"He was, doctor," the woman said. "But I think he's become delirious again."

"No!" Teddy said angrily. "I'm not delirious. I just have to find Tom." And then, as the realization of an awful possibility crept into his mind, he pleaded, "Why can't I see?"

Teddy heard the doctor say, "I have to talk to Private Nugent. Can you give us a few minutes?"

The nurse replied, "Certainly, Dr. McCrae. I'll see to some lads who will need dressings changed."

Dr. McCrae said, "Thank you, Nurse Bidwell."

Nurse Bidwell! Teddy remembered the picture of the young nursing sister his mother showed him in the photo album. He suddenly blurted out, "Nurse Bidwell! Please, don't go!"

"I'll be back later, Teddy," she said. Teddy heard the rustle of her clothing as she moved away, and then he knew she was gone.

"All of the lads in the ward love Nursing Sister Bidwell," Dr. McCrae said. "She'll take good care of you while you're here. Private Nugent . . ." Dr. McCrae paused, and Teddy heard him take a breath before continuing.

"You are very fortunate to be alive, Private Nugent . . . Teddy. Be thankful for that. You had a close call with an artillery shell. The blast knocked you unconscious. Stretcher-bearers picked you up; you were brought here by ambulance. You were much weakened by loss of blood, and you haven't been conscious for several days. I removed some shrapnel from your body, and the wounds will heal."

Something Joe had said about Nugent luck flashed into Teddy's mind but was instantly banished by that growing fear.

Dr. McCrae said, "Teddy, I'm going to roll back your blanket so you can use your hands. But before I do, I must tell you that you and all the other Canadian lads won a great victory. You took Vimy Ridge. Your country is proud of you."

Teddy didn't care that they had taken Vimy Ridge. He didn't care who was proud of him. He felt the blanket drawn down. His arms were free. But he was paralyzed with fear of what he was sure Dr. McCrea was going to tell him.

The doctor said, "Teddy, I want you to gently touch the bandage that is covering your eyes."

Teddy did so and felt gauze. "This is why I can't see," he said in a shaky voice. "If you take it off, will I be . . . jake?"

He heard Dr. McCrae take another deep breath.

"Your eyes were directly exposed to the hot, bright flash of the shell-burst. I'm sorry to have to give you bad news, Teddy. You must bear it like the brave soldier you are. Your eyes were burned and left completely sightless. The condition, I regret to say, is permanent."

"You mean I'm *blind*!" Teddy wailed.

Dr. McCrae simply said, "Yes." He took Teddy's hand in his and squeezed it.

Teddy pulled his hand away and cried, "NO! No, no, no!

This isn't right. I shouldn't even be here! I'm not a soldier, I'm just a kid. I want out of this dream. *I want to go home!*"

Teddy tried to push himself up from the bed. Dr. McCrae held him down and called out, "Nurse Bidwell! Your assistance, please."

She was there within moments. Teddy felt her hand take his as she said, "Oh, the poor lad."

There was no more struggle in Teddy. Drained of strength and wrapped in darkness, he sagged back onto the bed and lay there unmoving.

Dr. McCrae said, "Teddy? Private Nugent!"

Teddy didn't respond. He was fully conscious, but he didn't want to talk to anyone. He heard Nurse Bidwell say, "I think he's drifted off again, the poor dear. It's an evil war that does this to young men, Doctor."

Doctor McCrae said, "Yes, it is. But in desperate times, we have to fight. It's our duty, Nurse Bidwell."

Desperate! Once again, Teddy recalled what the old veteran had said. Dr. McCrae had just told him that he was permanently blind. Never in his life had he felt such fear, such desperation. In a loud voice, he said, "In Flanders fields the poppies blow between the crosses . . ."

Startled, Dr. McCrae said, "Teddy! You mustn't —"

"row on row that mark our place, and in the sky the larks . . ."

"Your poem, Dr. McRae. He's delirious again," Nurse Bidwell said. "Teddy, love, please —"

"still bravely singing, fly . . ."

Dr. McCrae and Nurse Bidwell were both talking to him, but their voices faded. Teddy could hear only his own words.

"scarce heard amid the guns below."

Then he felt as if he were floating in darkness. The last line he'd said echoed in his mind. He couldn't think of the next one.

"What's wrong with me? Why can't I remember it?"

He saw Joe and Tom, his parents and Ms. Potts. They were all telling him, "Come on, Teddy! You know the poem."

Then Paul and Valerie were there. Paul laughed and said, "Teddy forgot the poppy poem on the way to War Games."

Valerie huffed. And then Teddy saw her smile at him the way he liked to see her smile. The image melted away like a lost dream, and all of Teddy's sense of anything went with it.

3
The *Wolverine*

TEDDY HAD THE sensation that his bed was swaying back
and forth, like a swing in the park. At the same time, he had
the distinct feeling that he was being borne up, then suddenly
down and then up again, as though he was on the little kiddie
roller coaster at an amusement park. Back and forth, up and
down, over and over again. He'd had dreams about flying,
and even about leaping great distances like the Incredible
Hulk. But this was different. The motion felt real.

Teddy wanted to be in his own bed, but he was afraid he
was being transported from Dr. McCrae's hospital to some
institution for blind soldiers. He didn't want to even try to
open his eyes, fearful of the nothingness. The continuous
motion back and forth, up and down, rocked him like a baby

in a cradle. He wanted nothing more than to let it lull him back to sleep. But it didn't.

Instead, the ceaseless motion was making him nauseous. A cold shiver gripped him at the same moment that he broke out in a sweat. His head spun and his stomach felt queasy. Teddy shouted, "Nurse Bidwell! Hurry! I'm going to throw up!"

Then Teddy retched. A blast of vile-tasting gas rose up from his heaving stomach and belched out of his mouth. Instinctively, Teddy opened his eyes, threw off his blanket and tried to scramble out of bed so he could bolt for the bathroom. The bed swung out from under him, and he fell to the floor with a jarring thud.

Someone said, "There's a right way to get out of a hammock, but that isn't it."

The swaying had stopped, although Teddy could still feel himself going up and down, like in the wave pool of a water park. He was dizzy, but to his astonishment, he could *see*. There was no bandage over his eyes. He gasped, "I'm not blind!"

He heard somebody say, "Of course not. Seasickness never blinded anyone. Landsman!"

Teddy could have wept with relief that he wasn't actually blind, but once again he was bewildered. He'd been with Joe and Tom at Vimy Ridge, then in a hospital with Dr. John McCrae and Nursing Sister Bidwell — his own great-great-aunt. His last memory was of himself reciting "In Flanders Fields." He knew that the weirdness was at work again.

Teddy had hit the floor hard, but that didn't make him feel nearly as awful as the incessant up and down, up and down movement. He was flat on his back. A young man in a sailor's uniform was looking down at him, shaking his head. "Landsman!" he said again.

Teddy was about to ask, "Where am I?" Then he thought better of it and instead asked, "Who are you?"

"Well, I'm sure not Nurse Bidwell, whoever that is," the sailor replied. "Are you going to stay down there on the deck, or get up and get ready for your watch? Here, let me help you. I was seasick myself my first time out, but I've got my sea legs now. I'm Austin James, by the way. You can call me A.J."

With A.J.'s assistance, Teddy got up on wobbly legs and sat in a chair beside a long table. He saw that he was in a room not much larger than his bedroom. The few round windows were shut against water that sprayed against them. The door was also closed, but water seeped in at the bottom. A maze of pipes ran across the ceiling and walls. Among a dozen or so swinging hammocks, socks, underwear and other articles of wet clothing hung from some of the pipes. Teddy was certain he saw a few cockroaches skitter along the pipes. All around the room, flush against the walls, were big trunks with flat, padded tops. Between some of them were racks that held shoes, life jackets and other gear.

"That's my hammock you fell out of," A.J. said. "Seventeen men use this mess deck, and there isn't enough hammock space for everyone. New men have to bunk on the lockers. But you were in such a bad state after we sailed out of Halifax, I decided to lend it to you. Next time you bed down, it'll be on your locker. The trick is to hook an arm around a rack so you don't fall off when the sea gets rough. You're lucky. Most skippers have no sympathy for new lads who get seasick, but the Old Man on this corvette is a good sort. Gave me a couple of days to get my sea legs, and he's doing the same for you. Don't expect kindness like that from the other old salts, though. They aren't like me and the Old Man. Except Lieutenant Gordon. He's a good sort, too."

Teddy thanked A.J. for the use of his hammock but otherwise remained quiet while A.J. kept talking. He still felt horrible, but tried to focus on things A.J. said. *Halifax?* He had no recollection of being in that city or coming aboard a ship. *Just as he'd had no recollection of arriving in Tom and Joe's dugout.* Teddy knew that somehow, he'd awakened in a strange new place. But was he in yet another time? And what was a corvette? He realized that he was wearing a sailor's uniform just like A.J.'s. He also noticed gold-coloured lettering on a band around A.J.'s cap that said HMCS *Wolverine*.

A.J. lifted the lid of one of the trunks — which he said was his locker — and took out a can of peaches. As he opened it with a knife, he said, "You only let out that big belch because your belly was empty. If there'd been any food down there, you'd be wearing it now. Us old salts have a little trick for when the sea runs a bit heavy and you have a hard time keeping your grub down. Whenever you have leave to go ashore, buy tinned fruit and keep it in your locker. It's easier on your stomach than most of the stuff cook sends up from the galley."

A.J. plonked the can of peaches and a spoon on the table. Teddy had to grab them to keep them from sliding off as the ship rolled. "I'm not hungry," he moaned.

"I know," said A.J. "But you have to eat something. Try a little bit. If you have to puke, we keep a bucket under the table just for the occasion. Then you have to try again. That's how us old salts beat seasickness."

Teddy spooned up a piece of peach, put it in his mouth and swallowed. To his relief, it stayed down, so he tried one more, and then another. He started to feel a little better.

While Teddy ate the peaches, A.J. opened another can he'd taken from his locker. He sat across the table from Teddy and began spooning the contents into his mouth as though he enjoyed every morsel. Teddy thought it looked like dog food. He said, "That's not fruit."

"Mutton," said A.J. "Us old salts call it dog meat. Canned mutton, canned bully beef, canned ham, canned horse; we call it all dog meat. Mostly it's mutton. We get so much of this stuff, every sailor in the Royal Canadian Navy goes *baaa, baaa*."

Teddy was pleased with himself. Without asking any questions that might have made him seem dumb or even crazy, he'd learned that he was at sea on a Royal Canadian Navy ship called HMCS *Wolverine*. He thought that A.J. was only joking about the canned horse. He also felt A.J. was boasting a bit too much about being an "old salt." Teddy had seen that term in books, and he knew it referred to sailors who'd been at sea for many years. A.J. looked like he was about eighteen. Teddy didn't want to come right out and ask him how old he was. Instead, he asked, "What part of Canada are you from, A.J?"

"Edmonton, Alberta," A.J. replied.

Teddy slurped down a slice of peach and said, "Alberta is a long way from the ocean. Why did you join the navy?"

"Why did *you* join the navy?" A.J. asked back.

Teddy remembered his parents telling him about his great-grandfather David Steele, and said, "I come from a long line of navy men. You know, family tradition."

In the back of his mind, Teddy imagined Paul laughing and Valerie rolling her eyes.

"Well, your family tradition didn't help you much when we cleared Halifax Harbour for the open sea," A.J. said. "You were as seasick as any landsman I've ever seen. I joined the navy because I wanted to see faraway places. So far, all I've seen is Halifax, St. John's, Newfoundland . . . and Reykjavik. In case you never heard of it, that's the capital of Iceland. None of them are anything to write home about. But I guess I'll get to some really exciting ports eventually, if Jerry doesn't put a fish into us."

Teddy didn't want to ask A.J. who Jerry was or what he

meant by "a fish." So he said, "Is our captain a really old man?"

A.J. laughed and said, "For a fella from a long line of navy men, you sure don't know much. All sailors call their skipper the Old Man. It's like a tradition. It doesn't matter how old he is. Commander Steele, our skipper, is not an old man."

"*Steele?*" Teddy said. "*David* Steele?"

"That's the Old Man, all right," A.J. replied. "But lowly swabbies like us aren't on a first-name basis with the brass. To us, he's 'sir' or the 'Old Man.'"

"Of course. I know that," Teddy said. But he thought, *David Steele! My dad's grandfather! It must be him. How many David Steeles are navy officers?*

Teddy had seen his picture in the photo album, but he wasn't sure he'd recognize him if he saw him in person. If he did, he'd have to keep it to himself.

As Teddy ate the peaches and his nausea subsided, he became aware of a bad smell. He wondered why the places the weirdness took him to had to stink. "We could use a little fresh air in here," he said.

"We're lucky up here," A.J. said. "You should smell it down in the engine room. Bilge water, oil fumes and grease! And if you like it hot enough to sweat yourself down to your bones, go to the galley. The fragrance we have here comes from wet woollen socks, the paint locker next door and the build-up you get when we can't wash regularly because fresh water is rationed. You ever read that old poem that says 'Water, water everywhere, and not a drop to drink'? We're surrounded by seawater, but you can't wash in it. Most of the time we have to keep the door and the portholes closed or the sea comes pouring in, so the air gets pretty stale. If somebody gets seasick and barfs, the smell of it hangs around for a long time. We've got buckets, but the boys will like you better if you can make it to the rail to barf."

Teddy had just popped the last slice of peach into his mouth when the door suddenly opened. He saw the imposing figure of a man silhouetted against the grey daylight behind him. Sea spray struck him as he stood for a moment looking into the room. A big pale-green raincoat hid his uniform, but Teddy could tell from his peaked hat that he was an officer. The way he strode in, walking on the heaving deck as easily as if he were strolling along a sidewalk, told Teddy that he had what A.J. had called "sea legs."

A.J. immediately jumped up and snapped to attention. Teddy thought he was in the presence of Commander Steele — his great-grandfather. He still felt woozy, but he stood at attention and said, "I'm Teddy Nugent, sir. Are you the Old Man?"

The officer froze in his tracks. Teddy wondered how he could stand stock-still like that while the ship rolled with every wave. A.J. looked as though he wished he could die on the spot.

"I KNOW WHO YOU ARE, SEAMAN NUGENT!" the officer shouted in Teddy's face. "I AM LIEUTENANT GORDON, AND I DON'T RECALL GIVING YOU PERMISSION TO SPEAK!"

Teddy stiffened and gulped. He felt the heat in his face as he blushed. Lieutenant Gordon turned his attention to A.J.

"SEAMAN JAMES!" he snapped.

"SIR!" A.J. responded, looking straight ahead and not moving a muscle.

"How long have you been a seaman in the RCN?" Lieutenant Gordon asked. His voice was lower but his tone was still sharp.

"Four months, sir!" A.J. replied smartly.

"Four months. And yet you neglect to inform a landsman who never before felt the deck of a ship beneath his feet how to speak to an officer!" Lieutenant Gordon growled. Then he said, "Seaman Nugent, you're out of uniform."

Teddy was afraid to say a word, but his face showed his confusion. He *was* wearing a uniform.

"Your cap," the lieutenant said. "Why aren't you wearing it?"

Before Teddy could stammer a reply, A.J. said, "Permission to speak, sir?"

"Very well, Seaman James. Since Seaman Nugent doesn't seem to know why he isn't in compliance with regulations concerning the wearing of uniforms aboard one of His Majesty's Canadian ships of war, you tell me."

"Sir, when Seaman Nugent was laid low with seasickness, and I put him in my hammock — which I did with your kind permission, sir — I put his hat in his locker, sir," A.J. said.

"How long has Seaman Nugent been out of that hammock?" Lieutenant Gordon asked.

"About twenty minutes, sir," A.J. replied.

"So the two of you have had twenty minutes to sit here socializing and having a picnic of mutton and peaches, but no time to go to a locker for a hat. Do let me know how much time you'll need to get to your battle stations when we encounter a German U-boat. I'm sure that if we ask politely, Jerry will wait before he opens fire and sends us to the bottom. He might even be a good sport and take the time to ask Hitler for permission to sink us."

Hitler! Teddy suddenly understood what A.J. had been talking about earlier. "Jerry" meant the Germans. A "fish" was a torpedo fired by a U-boat, a German submarine. The weirdness had dropped him into World War II.

"The picnic is over," Lieutenant Gordon said. "Seaman Nugent, for your first watch aboard HMCS *Wolverine*, you're on rust patrol. Seaman James, you're going to show him what to do. I expect both of you to put some elbow grease into it. Now grab a couple of pommy-stones and get to it."

Minutes later, Teddy and A.J. were out on the ship's foredeck. Each had a black brick of volcanic pumice — a pommy-stone — for scraping away rust spots on metal surfaces and cleaning the wooden decks. As Teddy went to work, he soon realized it was a laborious task, hard on the back and the hands. He also realized that A.J. wasn't very happy.

"You're not supposed to say 'Old Man' to the officers," A.J. grumbled.

"I didn't know that," Teddy replied. Then he grumbled back, "You said Lieutenant Gordon is a good sort."

"He usually is," A.J. said. "But he's an officer, and sometimes they have to bark just to remind you that they're the top dogs."

Teddy had never been to sea. Valerie had once shown him photographs from a cruise holiday her family had taken in the Caribbean. Those pictures had been full of sunny skies and blue water and people having fun, nothing at all like what he could see from the deck of HMCS *Wolverine*.

In every direction Teddy looked, there was ocean. Huge, rolling hills of it! He found that a bit scary. The sky was overcast, with grey clouds hanging over green-grey water that swelled and fell. A strong wind whipped up whitecaps on the crests of the swells and blew spray into his face. It stung his eyes, and the drops that got into his mouth tasted salty. He knew he shouldn't be surprised, but he'd never tasted seawater before. He was glad of the raincoat A.J. had given him.

Then, through the spray and grey light, and over the heaving surface of the ocean, Teddy saw five other ships. They were in a long column, with wide gaps between them. He couldn't make out any details, except that they looked larger than the one he was on. Teddy could just make out the dark forms of another column some distance beyond them. "Who are they?" he asked A.J.

"Convoy," A.J. replied. "I think there's about forty of them this trip, but they're spread out. Freighters, tankers, troop carriers, all sailing for England. We're here to protect them from Jerry."

"What!" Teddy exclaimed. "This boat is supposed to protect forty ships?" It seemed absurd. He'd never seen anything like it in War Games strategy.

"This isn't a *boat*!" A.J. snapped, as though Teddy had just said something insulting. "She's a *ship*! A *boat* is what you get into to go from ship to shore. Like I said before, you sure don't know much about the navy."

"And being in the navy for just four months doesn't make you an old salt," Teddy shot back.

For a few minutes they continued scraping away at the deck without speaking. Teddy could see and hear other sailors going about their duties. Sometimes they called out to each other in terminology that was strange to him: fo'c'sle, gunnel, bulkhead. The only thing he heard several times that he understood was "Aye, aye, sir."

Everything on the ship that Teddy could see was unfamiliar. He might as well have been picked up by an alien spacecraft. He wanted to learn more about his situation, but he could tell that A.J. wasn't in the mood for annoying questions from a landsman. Then he saw a black cat dash out of a doorway and disappear around a corner.

"Was that a *cat*?" he asked.

"Oh, that's Dracula," A.J. said. "He's the ship's mascot. He's on full-time action station."

"Action station?" said Teddy. "A cat?"

"He kills rats," said A.J. "Everybody on board has an action station. That's his."

"What's your action station, A.J?"

As Teddy had hoped, A.J. began to come out of his sulk. "Well, I'm pretty good with electronics," he said. "When I'm not scraping rust because somebody said 'Old Man' to an officer, I'm assistant to the wireless operator. But we're on strict radio silence out here because Jerry can home in on transmissions, so the wireless doesn't get used much. So I'm learning to be an ASDIC operator."

"What's an ASDIC?" Teddy asked.

"Anti submarine detection device," A.J. explained. "The Yanks call it sonar. It's a system that uses sound waves to detect submarines and torpedoes underwater. If the crew in the ASDIC hut pick up on a U-boat, they estimate its location and then we drop depth charges on it. If they pick up on a torpedo, that might give us a few seconds to get out of its way."

Teddy didn't like the thought of having just a few seconds to escape being blown up by a torpedo. Now, the vast ocean seemed even more dangerous. He wondered if there could be U-boats out there right at that very moment, lurking beneath the waves. He asked A.J., "Have you ever detected a submarine?"

"No," A.J. replied. "So far, I haven't really been in any action with Jerry. But I did see some bodies from a freighter that got torpedoed. They were floating in a mass of wreckage. It was pretty awful, seeing those dead men and thinking that just before Jerry put a fish into their ship, they were alive and doing their jobs, just like us."

Some words flashed through Teddy's mind.

We are the dead. Short days ago

We lived, felt dawn, saw sunset's glow

Then A.J. seemed to brush the disturbing memory aside and said, "One time when I was listening on ASDIC, I thought I detected a torpedo. I told the leading seaman in the ASDIC hut, and he sounded action stations. The ship came about so hard she was almost on her beam end."

"What's that mean?" Teddy asked.

"It means the ship almost turned over sideways," A.J. said. "And the whole company from the bridge to the engine room braced for impact."

Teddy said, "So your warning saved the ship, right?"

"No," A.J. replied, sounding a bit embarrassed. "There was no torpedo. Just a waterlogged tree trunk that bumped into our hull and then floated away."

"Did you get in trouble for that?" Teddy asked.

"No," A.J. replied again. "Lieutenant Gordon said I did the right thing, because what if that log really was a torpedo. But some of the boys keep reminding me of it, if you know what I mean."

As they continued working, A.J. talked away. Teddy thought A.J. was still bragging, showing off how much he knew about the navy. He didn't mind, because A.J. was telling him things he needed to know, and he was glad A.J. was no longer mad at him.

"Of course, we're not the only ship guarding the convoy," A.J. said. "There are three other Canadian corvettes out there. Somewhere up ahead, there's a Royal Navy destroyer. The British sailors don't think much of us Canucks. You know, 'Britannia rules the waves,'" A.J. said in a mock British accent. "But they know Britain would be in deep trouble if Canada wasn't sending them all these shiploads of supplies."

Teddy learned that the corvettes were among the smallest warships in the RCN. The *Wolverine* was only two hundred feet long and thirty-three feet at the beam — the widest part. Seven officers and eighty crewmen made up the ship's company. The destroyer at the front of the convoy was more than three hundred feet long and carried two hundred and fifty men.

The *Wolverine* was armed with a four-inch gun, which A.J. explained meant that its shells were four inches in diameter. Three machine guns provided defence against enemy planes. The ship's principal weapons, A.J. said, were depth charges. Those were barrel-shaped bombs that could be launched by depth charge throwers or rolled into the sea on rails at the ship's stern.

"Nothing scares a Jerry in a U-boat more than depth charges," A.J. said. "One good blast close enough to the sub, and he's buried at sea." Then A.J. added, "And aircraft. The U-boats don't much like being surprised by planes that can bomb and strafe them."

"How can the pilots see the submarine if they're underwater," Teddy asked.

A.J. looked at Teddy and shook his head. "They don't stay underwater *all the time*," he said. "U-boats actually spend most of the time on the surface. They only go under when they're going to attack, or to escape being attacked themselves."

Teddy said, "So this convoy is protected by air force patrols as well as the navy ships, right?"

The idea of air cover fitted right in with Teddy's War Games experiences, and the thought of planes scaring U-boats away from the convoy made him feel a little more at ease.

But then A.J. said, "No. We're in the Black Pit."

Teddy didn't like the sound of that. "Black Pit?" he said. "What's that?"

"We're out of range of air patrols from Newfoundland," A.J. said. "There are hundreds of miles before we come into the range of the Royal Air Force. That's the Black Pit. It's where the U-boats can prowl with no danger of attack by aircraft. For all we know, a Jerry wolf pack could be watching us right now."

Teddy thought A.J. was just trying to scare him, the way Paul did sometimes when he thought he was being funny. But he couldn't help blurting out, "Wolf pack?"

"That's when a lot of U-boats get together to attack a convoy," A.J. said. "Just like a pack of wolves."

If the idea of one enemy U-boat made Teddy fearful, the

prospect of a whole fleet of them lying in ambush terrified him. He didn't ask A.J. any more questions because he was afraid of what he might hear. As he scrubbed the deck with his pommy-stone, feeling like he was accomplishing little for all his effort, he glanced about at the other sailors engaged in their activities. Why weren't they as afraid as he was? This ship wasn't like Tom and Joe's trench. There was no safe place if there was an attack, because any place of cover was on a ship that could sink into the cold, dark sea.

Although the ship pitched and rolled with every wave, the sea wasn't especially rough, at least according to A.J.

"It's the way these corvettes are built," he said. "I heard the bo's'n say that a corvette would roll on a field of wet grass. Just wait until we run into a heavy sea. Then you're *really* in for a ride."

Almost as if some sea god had overheard A.J., a sudden squall blew up. Rain poured down and the wind whipped across the water and buffeted the *Wolverine*, causing the ship to roll even more violently. The waves were higher, and the ship pitched forward and up and down at steeper inclines. Big rollers broke over the bow, leaving the deck awash. Teddy slipped and fell, and he slid down the deck as the ship plunged into a trough. He instantly forgot about the U-boats as he panicked and feared that he could be swept overboard. But then the deck suddenly shot up the other way, and Teddy slid back. A.J. grabbed him by the arm and pulled him to his feet. Then Lieutenant Gordon approached, navigating the treacherous deck as though his feet gripped it the way Spider-Man gripped walls.

"Seamen James and Nugent," he shouted above the wind and the crashing water, "Stow those pommy-stones and get to your mess deck."

The lieutenant turned away, shouted orders to some other sailors and went back the way he had come.

"I told you he was a good sort," A.J. said.

Minutes later, Teddy and A.J. were back in the room with the hammocks and lockers. It was crowded with sailors taking shelter from the squall. Some were in hammocks that swung like swings in a playground. Others sat on lockers and chairs, holding on to whatever they could so they wouldn't be thrown off by the roller-coaster motion.

The smell in the room was even worse than it had been, and Teddy quickly saw the source of the odour: the buckets that a few green-looking sailors clenched between their knees as they sat precariously on their lockers. The stench almost made him gag, but he managed to hold down the impulse to retch.

However, they'd been in the room but a few seconds when A.J. suddenly cried out, "MOVE!" He pushed his way past a couple of sailors and lurched toward one of the men with a bucket. He made it just in time.

"Blast it, A.J.!" the sailor grumbled. "Get your own puke pail."

Some of the men laughed.

"Sorry," A.J. gasped. "Blasted dog meat."

The men laughed again.

A.J. took a seat on a locker, and Teddy sat beside him. They both clung to the edge and braced their backs against the wall, which Teddy now knew was called a bulwark. Teddy quietly said to A.J., "You feeling better now, *Old Salt*?"

It was the kind of friendly teasing Teddy and Paul engaged in all the time. But within a few moments, Teddy wished he'd kept quiet.

One of the sailors said, "Now there's a good pair for you. Seaman Torpedo Tree James and Seaman Seasick Nugent. Hey, A.J., now that you got this lazy, seasick landsman out of your hammock, are you gonna show him how to find Jerry logs?"

A.J. winced at that, and some of the sailors laughed. But one of them with a bucket in his lap said, "Stow it, Morgan. The lad isn't the only one heaving his guts."

"Stow it?" Morgan shot back. "You telling *me* to stow it, Adams? How about I stow your face in that bucket!"

"You can try," Adams said. "I'm not so sick that I couldn't put *you* flat on the deck."

Teddy was afraid they were going to fight. A.J. didn't utter a word, so Teddy said to Adams, "Please, sir, it's okay. I don't ..."

Before he could finish, Morgan and most of the others burst into laughter. Teddy looked around in bewilderment, wondering what he'd said that was so funny. A.J. quietly told him, "You only say 'sir' to an officer."

Teddy felt the heat of embarrassment flush his face again.

Morgan said, "*Sir*! You hear that, Adams? You just got promoted. What are you now? Captain? If you're a captain, I'm an admiral. I'm making A.J. here senior officer in the ASDIC hut so he can log more logs in his log."

"Why don't you shut up!" A.J. growled. Morgan was laughing at his own joke, and he either didn't hear A.J. or just ignored him.

"Did you hear that, boys?" Morgan said, "Log more logs in his log!" He laughed louder and harder.

"ANOTHER WORD OUT OF YOU SAILOR, AND I'LL LOG YOU RIGHT INTO THE BRIG!"

Lieutenant Gordon stood in the doorway. The men on chairs and lockers jumped to attention while others tumbled out of their hammocks. Buckets clattered to the deck, spilling their contents. Most of the sailors managed to stand fairly straight on the heaving deck, but Teddy and a few others had to grasp something to keep from staggering. To the relief of all, Lieutenant Gordon told them to sit down — all but Morgan.

"We don't tolerate the harassment of any member of this ship's company," the lieutenant said. "You know that, Mr. Morgan. It stops now. Am I understood?"

"Aye, aye, sir! Understood!" Morgan replied sharply.

Lieutenant Gordon gave Morgan permission to sit and then looked away from him to speak to the men. As he did, Teddy was sure he saw Morgan glance at him and A.J. with a very unfriendly look. He thought for a moment that it was like the sinister glare of a pirate's eye.

"This squall won't last long," Lieutenant Gordon said. "As soon as she settles, I want this mess deck cleaned up. Seaman James, report to the ASDIC hut now."

As A.J. headed for the door, the lieutenant said, "Your usual vigilance, please, Seaman. The next log might be a torpedo."

A.J. looked around at the officer and said, "Aye, aye, sir." He was smiling as he went through the door.

"Seaman Nugent!" the lieutenant snapped. "Have you received any gunnery training?"

"No, sir," Teddy said. "I haven't. I —"

"A simple 'no, sir' will suffice, Seaman," Lieutenant Gordon interrupted. "What training in weapons operations *have* you received?"

Teddy stammered, "Well, sir, I . . . I don't know . . ."

"Never mind," the lieutenant said impatiently. "You're not the first rating the navy has sent me who doesn't know the bow of a ship from the stern. At O-six hundred tomorrow you will report to Gunner Morgan to begin instruction as part of his crew."

Teddy's heart sank. Gunner Morgan! Why did it have to be *him*? But he said, "Aye, aye, sir."

"Gunner Morgan will instruct you on handling ammunition and loading the weapon," Lieutenant Gordon said. "You will *not* fire the gun. If there should be a call to action stations, you will get the hell out of his way and stand by until you're ordered to do otherwise. Am I understood?"

"Yes, sir," Teddy said. "Understood."

The lieutenant then said to Morgan, "Commander Steele likes harmony and camaraderie among the crew. Don't disappoint him."

"No, sir. I won't," Morgan replied. "I'll take good care of Seaman Nugent, sir."

Something in the way Morgan said that made Teddy feel uneasy. Morgan clearly didn't like him, and now he was going to be part of Morgan's gun crew.

Teddy didn't like anything about this weirdness on a ship at sea in World War II. He hated the seasickness, the cold, the endless motion and the smell of the cramped quarters. Most of all, he hated the constant, nagging fear that at any moment a torpedo could hit his ship. How did A.J., Lieutenant Gordon, Adams and all the other men on the *Wolverine* stand it, day after day? Perhaps that's why some men, like Morgan, were so disagreeable.

"In the meantime, Seaman Nugent, I'm going to put you on U-boat watch," Lieutenant Gordon said. "Report to me on the bridge at seventeen-hundred."

Soon after Lieutenant Gordon left, the weather cleared up and the *Wolverine* was sailing on a calmer sea. Morgan thrust a mop into Teddy's hands and said, "You heard the lieutenant, *landsman*. He wants this mess cleaned up."

Teddy went to work with the mop and a bucket. As he held his breath and struggled not to slip in the mess, he frantically tried to figure out what 1700 meant. Then he recalled something he'd learned in geography class about international time. Instead of the day being divided into a.m. and p.m., there was a single twenty-four-hour period. One o'clock in the morning was 0100. Noon was 1200. One o'clock in the afternoon was 1300. Therefore, 1700 was five o'clock in the afternoon.

Teddy was pleased that he had figured it out by himself. With A.J. on duty in the ASDIC shed, he would have hated to ask someone else, like Morgan. Then his heart sank again when he realized that he would have to report to Morgan at six o'clock in the morning — after a night of trying to sleep on a locker, with his arm holding a rack, while U-boats skulked beneath the waves. Teddy's own bed, in his own house, in his own town on dry land had never seemed so inviting, so safe. He wished he was there, and he wondered if sailors like A.J. ever wished the same thing.

Teddy reported to the bridge on time. He knew it was the *Wolverine*'s command centre, like the bridge of the starship *Enterprise* in the old *Star Trek* TV show his dad liked to watch. But there were no computer screens, no banks of futuristic instruments that beeped and whirred. The only thing that Teddy recognized was the ship's steering wheel. All the other equipment had the look of old-fashioned, twentieth-century technology. Teddy could imagine Mr. Spock saying, "Primitive, but fascinating."

Lieutenant Gordon and several other officers and sailors were busy at various tasks, and Teddy thought no one had seen him enter. He said, "Seaman Nugent, reporting as ordered, sir."

"We see you, Seaman Nugent," said Lieutenant Gordon, who was studying a chart on a table with another officer. "We're not blind."

The other officer looked up at Teddy, who recognized him at once. David Steele — his great-grandfather — the *Wolverine*'s Old Man. Teddy managed to hide his astonishment at the same time that he suddenly recalled something his dad had said, that Steele had been in command of a ship that was sunk by a torpedo. *But surely not this ship*, he thought anxiously.

"Ah, yes, Seaman Nugent," the commander said, as if he and Teddy had already met, though Teddy was certain they hadn't. "Come over here, lad, and let me have a look at you."

Standing right in front of Commander Steele, Teddy thought there was something else familiar about him, but he couldn't place it.

"So, young man, how do you like being in the navy now?"

Teddy was tongue-tied. He couldn't admit that he didn't like being in the navy at all. He frantically searched for words. "Well, sir, I'm very sorry, but . . . well, I'm sorry to say that I've been —"

"Seasick!" Commander Steele said. "I know all about your illness, Seaman. You needn't apologize. It happens to all of us. But I wonder if you wish now that you'd volunteered for the army or the air force, eh! No seasickness or perils of the sea for those lads — at least, once we get them to England."

Teddy started to say, "No, sir, but —"

"But nothing," Commander Steele said. "Navy, army, air force — it doesn't matter which uniform you wear, lad, you do your part. But the war makes demands of everyone. We all pay, one way or another."

We all pay. . . . Then Teddy knew that Commander Steele was the old veteran in front of Mr. Singh's store! He looked younger here on the bridge of HMCS *Wolverine* sometime in the 1940s, but it was definitely him. Teddy stifled the urge to blurt something out about that poppy. He stood quietly while the commander continued.

"Part of your price, son, was a bout of seasickness." Then Commander Steele gave Teddy a little cuff on the shoulder and said, "But now you've got your sea legs, eh? Ready to show Jerry what Canadians are made of?"

For a moment, Teddy didn't understand that he was supposed to respond. Then he said, "Yes . . . I mean, aye aye, sir."

Commander Steele said, "Right, then. He's all yours, Mr. Gordon."

As the commander turned his attention back to his chart, Teddy thought, *I'm yours, too, sir. More than you know.*

Seconds later, Teddy and Lieutenant Gordon stood at a rail outside the entrance to the bridge. The lieutenant had a pair of binoculars in his hand. From this position high above the main deck, they could see the whole bow section of the ship and the wide ocean in every direction except behind them.

"You're on U-boat watch," Lieutenant Gordon said. "Listen closely to what I tell you."

"Excuse me, sir," Teddy said, "but I thought —"

"I said *listen closely*, Seaman Nugent," the lieutenant said sharply, cutting Teddy off. "You were about to ask me why, if we have ASDIC, you're on U-boat watch with binoculars. ASDIC can't detect a U-boat when it's on the surface or only at periscope depth. No matter how deep it hides, it has to come close enough to the surface for the Jerry captain to raise his periscope for a look around. That periscope is what you're looking for."

Lieutenant Gordon showed Teddy how to use the binoculars as he explained the duty.

"You're going to make a ninety-degree sweep from dead-ahead to starboard, back to dead-ahead, and then ninety degrees to port and back to dead-ahead. Not too quickly. You will keep doing that until you're relieved of this watch. Scan every foot of water, and don't even blink. That periscope you're watching for is hard to spot, but it leaves a wake that gives it away if you keep a sharp eye. If you see *anything* that looks suspicious, note its position and then open this door and report immediately. Don't wait to be spoken to. Am I understood?"

"Understood, sir," Teddy said.

Lieutenant Gordon went back inside, and Teddy began to scan the sea as he'd been instructed. All he could see was rolling water. He found that the ship's motion carried his gaze to and fro as he swept the binoculars from side to side. He felt a twinge of excitement at the thought of spotting a periscope. If he actually caught sight of the enemy, he'd be a hero.

But what if he only *thought* he saw a periscope and gave an alarm that turned out to be false? Then he'd get the ridicule Morgan and some of the others gave A.J. over the log. Teddy's mind was in a turmoil over the whole situation. If he saw a periscope, it meant that there really was a U-boat down there. But if he didn't see a periscope, it didn't necessarily mean there was no U-boat, only that he hadn't seen the periscope. That was frightening. Hadn't some famous director of scary movies said that it's what you *can't* see that is the scariest of all? And hadn't that same director said that when a movie audience sees a bomb under an unsuspecting character's chair, it is *they* who are afraid, not the person sitting in the chair. Teddy felt like he was both the potential victim and a watcher in the audience because he knew that Commander Steele had lost a ship. He just didn't know if it would be the *Wolverine*.

Sometimes the rise and fall of Teddy's line of vision through the binoculars brought convoy freighters into view. He caught glimpses of sailors moving about on them. They were civilians, not navy men, but their job was every bit as dangerous. *Their* ships were the U-boats' main targets. Teddy resisted the temptation to take a few seconds for a really good look at them. He didn't want to make a mistake on U-boat watch.

After about fifteen minutes, Teddy's neck began to hurt. More minutes passed, and the ache spread to his shoulders and arms. He kept his upper body moving, starboard to port and back, with his feet firmly in one place. A new pain began to burn in the small of his back. He wiggled the fingers holding the binoculars to fight the numbness creeping into them and wished he'd asked Lieutenant Gordon for gloves. Peering through the lenses without a moment's break was making his eyes bleary. Teddy didn't dare take the binoculars away from his face in case Lieutenant Gordon — or even worse, Commander Steele — saw him through the window. But in spite of his effort not to, he blinked. Surely, he thought, they couldn't see *that*.

The monotony of Teddy's watch was shattered by a sea-shaking explosion. The sound of the blast that ripped through the grey North Atlantic dusk made Teddy jump and almost drop his binoculars. About half-a-mile off the *Wolverine*'s starboard bow, one of the convoy's ships, an oil tanker, was on fire. Teddy recovered his grip on the binoculars and trained them on the stricken ship. To his horror, he could see men leap from the burning vessel into the sea. He was sure he could hear their cries coming across the water.

There was another explosion, ten times louder than the first, and a ball of fire fuelled by thousands of gallons of petroleum burst skyward, illuminating the clouds in a hellish red and yellow light. Then the sea itself was on fire as the doomed tanker disgorged its cargo.

Off in the distance there was another flash, followed moments later by an ear-splitting BANG, like the clap of thunder after a bolt of lightning. Then a fourth, from a different direction. Teddy's worst fear had come true. The convoy was under attack by a wolf pack.

The *Wolverine*'s horn shrieked the alarm and sailors rushed to their action stations. Lieutenant Gordon was suddenly beside Teddy. He grabbed the binoculars from him. Teddy panicked. Was this happening because he'd blinked?

"I'm sorry, sir," Teddy cried. "I didn't see a periscope!"

"I know that, blast it!" the lieutenant barked as he snatched a look at the sinking tanker. "Nobody did! Report to Gunner Morgan. . . . NOW, Seaman Nugent!"

Teddy ran down to the main deck and hurried toward the companionway that would take him to the gun manned by Morgan's crew. In his rush, he collided with A.J., who was going the opposite way.

"A.J.! Did the ASDIC find the U-boats?" Teddy asked anxiously.

"Didn't pick up on anything until it was too late!" A.J. said hurriedly. "There are three that we know of. Maybe more. It's a blasted wolf pack. I've gotta report to the bridge."

Then A.J. was gone. Teddy raced to the machine gun emplacement that overlooked the ship's stern section. Morgan and three other sailors were readying the weapon for action. Teddy lost his balance and fell as the *Wolverine* made a sudden hard turn to starboard.

"Blast it, Nugent!" Morgan shouted. "Don't you know enough to hang on to something! If you go overboard, nobody is gonna stop to pick you up. Not while Jerry is out there. And where in blazes is your Mae West?"

Teddy didn't know what Morgan was talking about. "My *what*?" he asked.

Morgan said, "Your Mae . . . Oh, for pity's sake! Your life jacket!"

Only then did Teddy notice that Morgan and his crew were wearing things that didn't look like any life jackets he'd ever seen. A.J. had been wearing one, too.

"I don't have one, sir," Teddy said.

"I'm not a *sir*, you seasick landsman," Morgan barked. Then he pulled off his life jacket and thrust it into Teddy's hands. "Put that on," he ordered.

Surprised, Teddy said, "But . . . this is yours."

"It's not mine, it's the navy's," Morgan replied impatiently. "And so are you. I'll get another one. Now put it on. Pull that cord if you have to inflate it"

Teddy slipped the life jacket over his head but didn't know how to fasten the straps. Morgan spat out a few words that would have gotten Teddy in trouble if his parents or Ms. Potts ever heard *him* say them. Then the gunner, who Teddy had thought didn't like him, fastened him in.

"What do you want me to do?" Teddy asked as Morgan pulled the last strap so tight it made him wince.

"Just keep out of our way," Morgan said. "And try not to fall overboard. Even with the Mae West on, you'll soon freeze to death in these waters."

Teddy stepped back and grasped a railing. He was scared, but he wished he could do something useful.

Then, as if he'd read Teddy's mind, Morgan said, "You see

the barrels those sailors are loading into the port and starboard launchers? Those are depth charges. Those are what we use to kill U-boats. Our gun won't go into action unless Jerry is forced to surface and tries to shoot it out with us. If that happens, I might need you to run to the magazine and have them send more ammunition. So be ready. Understood?"

"Understood!" Teddy said.

Morgan gave instructions to the three men in his gunnery crew: McGean, Jackson and Freeman. The sound of another explosion rolled across the sea as yet another ship was torpedoed. It was dark now, and the ships of the convoy and their other naval escorts were almost invisible to Teddy because they sailed with no lights that would make them easy targets. The overcast sky meant they wouldn't be silhouetted in moonlight or against the star-filled heavens. But the glow from ships on fire and the inferno of burning oil reflected off vessels as they passed in and out of sight like ghost ships.

The *Wolverine* pitched and plunged on an erratic course, surging dead ahead, turning sharply one way and then turning sharply again in another direction. Teddy was sure they must have picked up on a U-boat with the ASDIC and were closing in as the sub tried to give them the slip. He clung to the rail as the corvette heaved over from one side to the other, keeping after the enemy like a bloodhound on a trail.

Teddy heard officers on the deck below him shout orders. Four depth charges catapulted from the *Wolverine*. They arced skyward and then plunged into the sea. Moments later, geysers of water erupted with a noise like muffled thunder. *WHUMP, WHUMP, WHUMP, WHUMP!*

"Take *that*, Jerry!" Morgan yelled.

From across the water came the sounds of the strange battle between the surface ships and the submerged wolf pack. The sharp blast of a torpedo striking a victim was followed by the muted explosions of depth charges as the prowling U-boats became the hunted.

Then Morgan cried out, "TORPEDO! STARBOARD BOW!"

Teddy looked, and his eyes went wide. He couldn't see the torpedo, just the churning silvery wake its propeller made as it streaked just below the surface, straight at the *Wolverine*. The corvette careened hard to port, but the evasive manoeuvre was too late. The torpedo struck the *Wolverine* amidships on the starboard side and exploded. The impact, combined with the momentum of the sharp turn, almost forced the small warship over onto the port beam.

Teddy's hands were torn from their grip on the rail and he was thrown through the air. He instinctively braced himself for a hard landing on the main deck. Instead, he was stunned by a frigid shock as he plunged into dark water. The sudden cold knocked the breath out of him and he sucked in seawater. He felt himself going down as he thrashed his arms and kicked his legs. Then he remembered the cord on his life jacket. He groped frantically, found it and pulled hard. The sudden buoyancy of the life jacket yanked him to the surface so violently that the straps bit through his clothing and into his skin.

Teddy's head broke the surface. He gasped for air and got another mouthful of seawater. To his alarm, he saw that the *Wolverine* was already far from him. The corvette was listing as water poured into the hole the torpedo had blasted through the hull. Teddy knew the *Wolverine* was finished.

Held up by his life jacket but already numb from the icy water, Teddy saw fires break out on the doomed ship. The light cast by the flames across the surface revealed men bobbing up and down in the water — crew members who'd been thrown overboard or had jumped into the sea to escape the flames.

The sailors in the water called out to each other. Teddy heard men respond to their names. Among them were Morgan's men: McGean, Jackson and Freeman. One of them shouted, "Morgan?"

There was no reply. Another called Morgan's name and got no answer. Teddy heard one say, "He went into the water with the rest of us. I saw him."

Someone else said, "Morgan didn't have his Mae West. He gave it to Nugent."

Teddy felt sick and not from the seawater he'd swallowed.

"Nugent?" a voice called. "Nugent, you out there?"

A pang of guilt as sharp as the water was chilling gripped Teddy. It made him reluctant to answer. But he did.

"Yes," he shouted. "I'm here." The response he got wasn't what he expected.

"Don't be afraid, lad. Find a piece of wreckage to hold onto. They'll get life boats away before the *Wolverine* goes down. They'll find us. Keep your arms and legs moving. Keep shouting."

Then Teddy understood. A sailor's responsibility to his shipmates swept aside personal feelings and quarrels. They relied on each other for survival.

But even as the sailor called out, the sound of his voice trailed away as the merciless sea carried him and Teddy farther apart. Then it was lost in the din of the battle. Teddy found no floating debris to hold onto. He kept his arms and legs moving to fight the cold that crept into the very core of his body. Even that didn't match the cold that had seized his heart and spirit.

Was Morgan dead because of him? What about A.J.? And Lieutenant Gordon and Commander Steele? Did they get away in the lifeboats? Or were their bodies floating on the water like those other unlucky men A.J. had told him about?

Teddy shouted "Hello," again and again. No one answered. His struggle to stay alive in the middle of the Atlantic Ocean was exhausting. Where was that lifeboat from the *Wolverine*? A.J. might be in it, looking for him.

There was no feeling in Teddy's arms and legs. He wasn't even sure if they were still moving. He was shivering so badly that his teeth chattered. Teddy felt drowsiness come over him and was surprised at how comforting it felt — almost like a warm blanket. It would be good to sleep for just a little while and get some of his strength back. He was dimly aware that the world around him had grown quiet— no more sounds of ships' engines or explosions.

Then the ceiling of cloud broke and the ocean surface was awash in moonlight. Teddy couldn't see any ships. He shook his head to cast off the sleepiness and made his leaden arms turn him around in the water so he could look in every direction. Not a ship to be seen anywhere! The convoy had left him behind. There would be no lifeboat.

Teddy was alone in a vast emptiness of sea and sky with nothing but the moon, the stars and a few passing rags of cloud for company. But not entirely alone. Something bumped the back of his head.

Teddy turned himself around again, hoping it was a piece of debris from a stricken ship he could grab hold of; maybe it would be big enough for him to drag himself onto and get out of the water. But he recoiled at what he saw just inches from his face. A body!

With a surge of strength Teddy hadn't thought he still had in him, he pushed the dead man away. The corpse was floating face down with only the back visible above the water. In the pale light, Teddy could see that it wasn't wearing a navy uniform. The drowned man had been a merchant sailor, a victim of a U-boat attack on one of the convoy's freighters.

"Never had a chance," Teddy thought. "Just doing a job, and then *boom*! You're dead."

Then the words came to him, the lines he hadn't been able

to remember. It seemed such a long time ago. He said them, spitting out the seawater that sloshed into his mouth. "We . . . are the . . . Dead. Short . . . days ago, we lived . . . felt dawn . . . saw . . . sunset glow . . . loved . . . and were . . . loved, and . . . now . . . we lie . . . in Flanders fields."

No sooner had Teddy uttered the last three words than he felt himself caught in a whirlpool. It spun him around and around. Then, in spite of his Mae West, it pulled him down into watery darkness. As Teddy whirled about in the vortex, he saw his parents reaching out to him. He wanted to grasp their hands, but his arms were stretched above his head, uselessly reaching for the surface, and he couldn't move them.

Then his mom and dad were gone, and Paul was there. He grinned and said, "Round and round Teddy goes. Where he comes down, nobody knows. Just joking, Ted."

Paul disappeared and Valerie appeared. "No cheating allowed," she said. "Grow up, Teddy."

Valerie faded away and was replaced by Ms. Potts. "Not all the dead are in Flanders fields, Teddy Nugent," she said. "The sea is a graveyard, too."

Then she was gone, and Teddy was shrouded in an inky black abyss of loneliness.

4
Bomber Command

●

"WAKE UP, NUGENT! Come on, old boy, shake a leg."

Teddy awakened with a start and gasped, "A.J.?"

But he knew at once that the British-sounding voice wasn't A.J.'s. He wasn't in the water, and he wasn't in the *Wolverine*'s lifeboat. This time, Teddy didn't even dare to wonder if at last he was back home in his own bed. He knew without thinking that the weirdness had taken him to another place and time. The bed he lay on was narrow and hard. The blanket that covered him had an unpleasant smell, something like his camping sleeping bag when it hadn't been washed for a long time. The man standing above him wore a uniform, but it wasn't like the one worn by Tom and Joe or any of the men on the *Wolverine*. Nonetheless, Teddy could tell that the man was an officer. A moment after saying A.J.'s name, Teddy said, "Sir?"

"No, not 'A.J., *sir*,'" the officer said. "It's Captain Bidwell, *sir*! Was this A.J. your training officer? It seems he neglected to instruct you on how to properly address a Royal Air Force officer. That's been a bit of a problem with you Canadians. But don't worry. We'll shape you up quickly enough. Now get on your feet, Air Gunner Nugent. You're on the list for tonight's Battle Order, and you've been assigned to my bomber."

Bidwell again! Teddy thought as he threw off the blanket and jumped out of bed. *Mom's family! The bomber pilot! MY GREAT-GRANDFATHER! Everybody says I have Mom's eyes. He has her eyes, too. No, she has* his *eyes. And his nose, too. I have that nose. But not the moustache. Neither does Mom. And why did he call me an air gunner?*

Teddy stood up. He wasn't surprised to find that he was dressed only in undershorts and an undershirt, but he noticed that the latter was an old-fashioned garment with no sleeves.

"AT ATTENTION!" Captain Bidwell barked.

Teddy snapped to attention. Looking straight ahead, he could see only part of the room. It was enough for him to realize he was in some sort of barracks. He saw a row of cots like the one on which he'd awakened. The wooden walls were painted a dingy green. Behind the captain was an open door and above it a photograph of an officious-looking man in a military uniform. Teddy recognized the two small flags that flanked the picture. One was the British Union Jack. The other was the old flag of Canada — the one that had been replaced by the Maple Leaf flag before Teddy was born.

Sounds of activity came through the door — a garble of talk mixed with shouted orders, curses and snatches of subdued laughter. Overriding all of it was a loud hum that reminded Teddy of Saturday mornings in summer when his father and the neighbours attacked the grass in their yards with lawn mowers. Whenever Teddy had to mow the lawn, he would plot the job like a War Games campaign. But the lawn mower noise was never like that which he was hearing now. Not as loud, and not as constant.

"Gunner Nugent," Captain Bidwell said with a sigh and a shake of his head. "I know that out here on the airfields we aren't always as stringent about regulations as we might be, but all of us, including you Canadians, WILL SALUTE A SUPERIOR OFFICER!"

Teddy's right hand flashed up to his forehead. He found the captain's tendency to speak softly one moment and yell at him the next unnerving. He guessed that was probably the intent.

"Very good, old boy," said the captain. "Now, be a good chap and keep your hand there until I tell you to stand at ease. I've only got a few minutes to spare for you, so do pay attention."

Captain Bidwell folded his arms behind this back and walked up and down in front of Teddy as he spoke.

"I'm going to turn you over to my wireless operator, Sergeant Lynne, so he can show you around a bit before briefing. But I always like to meet a new crew member personally before we go on a mission. Since you didn't arrive with the other replacements until late last night, I'm doing that now."

Teddy didn't like the sound of that word, *replacements*. *Like when I replaced poor Charlie in the trench*, he thought. *What happened to the man I'm replacing?*

"I like to have a happy crew, and I think the other chaps will tell you I'm not a hard officer to get along with," Captain Bidwell said. "But up there, we all depend on each other. Like Lord Nelson said at Trafalgar, I expect every man to do his duty.

"As you are no doubt aware, the RAF has been flying night-time bombing raids over Germany and occupied territory, giving Hitler a taste of what he's been doing to us. The Luftwaffe takes exception to that and sends its Messerschmitts up to stop us. Not every bomber that leaves England makes it back. And some of those that do, have casualties among the crews. Our British lads have been spread a bit thin, so lads like you from the colonies — Canada, Australia, New Zealand and South Africa — and some foreign airmen who escaped occupied countries have been sent to help us fill the ranks."

Teddy *really* didn't like the sound of that. Captain Bidwell must have read something in his face, because he said, "I've flown more than twenty missions, and I haven't lost a man yet. Don't worry, Nugent. The crew member you're replacing came down with food poisoning."

Teddy wondered if the Royal Air Force served its men the same canned "dog meat" the Royal Navy fed its sailors. His right arm was starting to ache and his hand felt a little shaky. Captain Bidwell continued talking without saying he could stand at ease.

"I'm telling you all this because you'll be flying your first mission over enemy territory tonight, and I don't want you to have any misconceptions about what lies ahead. Forewarned is forearmed, and all that. You'll be in the dorsal gun turret. We'll have fighter plane escort over the Channel and for the first part of our course over France, but once we're out of the fighters' range, we're on our own. It will be up to you gunners to keep the bloody Nazi night-fighters off our back.

"It gets cold up there, Nugent. Especially in the gun turrets. I know you Canadians love the cold, but nonetheless you'll do well to put on a woollen jumper before boarding the aircraft. Can't have your teeth chattering while you're trying to shoot down a Nazi fighter, can we?"

A young man in an RAF uniform entered the room. He halted just a step inside the door, stood at attention, saluted smartly and said, "Sergeant Lynne reporting as ordered, sir!"

Captain Bidwell said, "Ah, there you are, Lynne. Spot on time. I'll leave our brave Canadian to you."

"Very well, sir," Lynne responded.

Captain Bidwell started for the door but then stopped as though he'd just remembered something. "By the way, Lynne," he said, "I'd think it awfully good of you to show Nugent the correct way to salute in the Royal Air Force. He's been standing in front of me and our portrait of His Majesty King George making a Boy Scout salute. You may stand at ease now, Nugent. Good morning, gentlemen."

As the captain left the room, Teddy lowered his arm in relief. He asked Lynne, "Do I have permission to speak, sir?"

Lynne laughed and said, "Oh, blimey! *Sir?* You *are* a babe in the woods, ain't you? Look, when Biddy or any other officers are about, you 'ave to call me sergeant. But when it's just you and me and the flowers and bees, call me Mel. Not *Melvin*, mind you. I'll call you Ted. Or is it Edward or Theodore?"

"Ted!" Teddy replied.

"Right, then," Mel said. "It's in me 'ead that your name is Ted. The first thing you've got to do, me ol' duck, is get into your uniform. Can't go out on the field looking like your dear ol' mum forgot to dress you."

In a locker at the foot of his cot, Teddy found a uniform: socks, boots, pants, shirt, a formal-looking jacket that Mel called a tunic and a side-cap like the one Mel wore. There was also a woollen sweater, the "jumper" Captain Bidwell had mentioned.

"Be a bit 'ot if you put that on now," Mel said. "Loverly warm day like this, the other blokes won't put the woollies on until flight time. Otherwise they'd be sweating gumdrops."

Teddy glanced at the row of cots and asked, "Where are the other . . . blokes?"

"They're up and about," Mel said. "You ain't the first new bloke to sleep through reveille. If I know these lads, they'd 'ave given you a jolly good rousting, but I suspect Biddy sent them on their way so you and 'im could 'ave a private consultation about war strategy."

As Teddy got dressed, Mel said, "So . . . you're *Can-ie-dian*. Me older brother Arthur emigrated to Canada before the war. Took 'is missus and kids to Toronto. Arthur Lynne. Any chance you met 'im?"

"No," Teddy replied. "I'm not from Toronto." He had the impression that Mel didn't know how big Canada was.

Teddy had heard English accents before, but there was something different about Mel's. He didn't sound like Captain Bidwell or any of the British actors Teddy had heard in the movies.

"Where are you from, Mel?" he asked. "I mean, where in England? London?"

"London indeed, mate," Mel said, with a clear note of pride. "I came into this world within the sound of the bells of St. Mary-le-Bow in the East End. That makes me a true Bow-Bells Cockney lad. Me ol' dad's a barrow boy. Lost an eye fightin' the Kaiser in the Great War, 'e did. Says 'e's only blind when 'e winks. Most of my lot went into the army when 'itler started with 'is bleedin' big box o' toys. But I didn't want to muck around in the dirt like me dad, and I didn't fancy tossin' up me gravy in the navy. So I took instruction to be a wireless operator in the RAF. And 'ere I am, at your service."

Teddy didn't understand everything he'd just heard. But he decided that he liked Mel. In some ways, the young Englishman reminded him of Joe, Tom, A.J. and even a little of Paul.

Teddy noticed the insignia that was sewn above the left breast pocket of his tunic. It looked something like the winged-wheel crest of the Detroit Red Wings National Hockey League team. The insignia had a gold-coloured wing and the letters AG. Mel's tunic had the same insignia, but on his sleeve was a patch with lightning bolts that Teddy's uniform didn't have.

Teddy had learned from previous experiences that his questions could sound dumb. This time, he saw a way around that problem. He would employ a little War Games strategy to gain information.

Teddy said, "Mel, I hope you don't think I sound silly asking you this —"

"Not at all, mate," Mel interrupted. "Fire away."

"Well, the patches on these RAF uniforms are different from the ones on Canadian uniforms," Teddy said. "I think I ought to know what they mean."

"Right you are," Mel said. "Which reminds me, I 'aven't shown you the proper RAF salute like Biddy said I should. You do it like this."

Mel demonstrated the salute, which was not like the three-fingered Boy Scout salute Teddy had used because it was one he'd seen on TV. It was the same one Mel had made when he entered the room, but Teddy hadn't paid attention then to just how rigidly Mel stood and how his hand practically quivered when he snapped it to his forehead. Mel told Teddy to do it and then had him repeat the action three times.

"Got to be sure you 'ave it right," Mel said. "Some of these officers go bloody bonkers if you're just a twitch off. Now that we 'ave that vital contribution to the war effort out of the way and 'itler is tremblin' in 'is boots, what d'you want to know?"

"Those flashes on your sleeve," Teddy said. "What do they mean?"

"My sparks?" Mel said, touching a finger to the patch on his arm. "These little darlin's tell one and all that I'm a wireless operator. I also look after the Airborne Interception Radar set that detects Jerry night-fighters. And these stripes 'ere mean that I 'ave the rank of sergeant. That don't mean that I get to yell orders at anybody, except maybe you. But it could come in 'andy if we get shot down and Jerry takes me prisoner. Supposedly, they give non-coms — that's sergeants like me — and officers a bit better treatment than ordinary enlisted men."

"Shot down!" Teddy said, not liking the sound of the words at all. "What happens to *me* if I'm captured?"

"Just 'ope we don't get shot down," Mel replied.

Teddy suddenly had a queasy feeling in his stomach, something like what he'd experienced on the *Wolverine*. But there was no heaving deck under his feet now, and he managed to hide his discomfort.

"These wing patches on our tunics," Teddy said, "What does AG stand for?"

"Air Gunner," Mel replied.

"But you're a wireless operator," Teddy said. "Why do you have an air gunner patch?"

"Because I'm an indispensable bloke of many trades," Mel said. "Most of the time that we're over enemy territory, we're under radio silence. I only get on the ol' sparky if there's an emergency situation. King Georgie, bless 'is little 'eart, might think lads like me ain't earnin' our shilling if we just lay about like we was on 'oliday. So I'm an air gunner, too. I'm the bloke in the nose turret. When the Jerry marauders start buzzin' around us like flies, you get to shoot at the ones I miss."

Teddy felt that queasy feeling again. He almost asked Mel if firing the turret guns was anything like shooting down planes in a video game. But of course, Mel wouldn't know what a video game was. And Teddy knew without asking that firing a real gun at real planes that were shooting back was no game.

"There you are, dressed to the nines and right on time," Mel said when Teddy stood before him in his uniform.

"Nines?" Teddy said.

"It means you look smashin'," Mel replied. "Blimey, but you're going to 'ave to learn to talk proper English, mate. Now let's get a bite o' grub. I don't know about you, but I could do with a cuppa, a bit of borrow-an'-beg and a bowl of 'orse feed. If we're lucky, there'll be some satin-an'-silk to pour on it."

Teddy had no idea what Mel was talking about.

Outside, Teddy saw that they were in a compound of oddly shaped buildings identical to the one he'd just been in. They were semi-cylindrical, almost like big barrels laying on their sides with curved metal roofs that went all the way to the ground.

When Teddy commented on the unusual structures, Mel said, "Blimey! What do you 'ave for barracks in Canada? Igloos? These are Nissen 'uts. They're 'ome sweet 'ome to RAF lads from 'ere to Scotland. They ain't exactly Buck'nam Palace, but the loverly thing about 'em is that they're all the same. Wherever a bloke gets posted 'ere in ol' Blighty, 'e can always kip in surroundings 'e knows and loves."

"Kip?" Teddy said.

"Sleep," Mel replied with an impatient shake of his head.

The sound of an engine caught Teddy's attention. He looked up and saw a plane approaching. It was descending, and the closer it came, the louder the roar of the engine. The aircraft swept overhead and Teddy could clearly see the red, white and blue roundel of the Royal Air Force on the underside of each wing.

"Spitfire returning from patrol. The airfield is just over that way," Mel said, pointing in the direction.

"Don't they have mufflers?" Teddy asked.

"That noise is nothin'," Mel replied. "You should 'ear those Nazi Stuka dive-bombers when they come screamin' down at you! On second thought, maybe you shouldn't. Might be the last thing you ever 'ear."

As Mel led him through the base, Teddy saw that he was in yet another bewildering world in which there was little that he recognized or understood. He was thankful that Mel felt it necessary to explain everything to the Canadian newcomer.

"That up there on that Eiffel Tower is the air-raid warning siren," Mel said. "We call it Big Ben. If it goes off, you run for cover. If you can't find a place to 'ide, squat down, stick your fingers in your ears, shut your eyes tight and 'ide under your 'at. Don't worry about your plane. That's the pilot's job."

"Air raid!" Teddy exclaimed, looking up into a clear blue sky. He suddenly felt the same fear that had struck him when he'd been told about the U-boats. "Does that happen very often?"

"Don't get so excited, Ted me ol' mate," Mel said. "We know Jerry's comin' before 'e gets 'ere. Anyway, they don't come as often in the daytime anymore. Our Spitfires and 'urricanes are too much for 'em. But if that siren goes off, you move fast, just in case."

They walked past a field where Teddy saw men playing what he first thought was baseball. Then he realized it was a different game.

"What are those guys playing?" he asked.

"That's cricket," Mel said, surprised that Teddy should

even ask. "Ain't you never seen it? Oh, right! You *Caniedian* lads play ice 'ockey. I guess that's a right enough game for over there. Be pretty 'ard for you to play a civilized game like cricket wearin' ice skates on a frozen lake."

The word *civilized* grated on Teddy. Had Mel just poked fun at him? Teddy was about to speak up in defence of hockey when Mel said, "Well, 'ere we are. Beyond this door is the finest dining in England. Mr. Churchill and the royal family are reg'lar customers."

Teddy and Mel entered a long wood-frame building that stood out from the surrounding Nissen huts. It was rectangular, with regular walls and a conventional sloped roof. Teddy saw tables at which a few men sat eating, and a serving counter. The smell of food that reached his nose and chased away the queasiness in his stomach told him he was in some sort of cafeteria. Mel called it the canteen.

Teddy was hungry. The last thing he could recall eating was A.J.'s canned fruit on the *Wolverine*. He wondered if he was about to get a serving of the notorious mutton. What he got was even less appetizing.

When Teddy sat down at a table with Mel, he had before him a tray with a plate, a bowl and a cup. On the plate was a yellowish blob that looked like mushy mashed potatoes. It was powdered eggs — what Mel had called "borrow-and-beg." The "horse feed" in the bowl was a gluey lump of oatmeal. Teddy didn't think it was much improved by the tiny ration of canned milk he was given, but Mel seemed pleased with his little serving of "satin-an'-silk." He saved a few drops for his "cuppa" — his cup of tea — and wished aloud that he had a bit of sugar.

"Bloody rationing!" Mel grumbled. "Every flippin' thing is in short supply. You know, Jamaica, where sugar comes from, is a British colony. You'd think we'd 'ave lots of it. But them lousy rotten U-Boats keep sinkin' the ships that bring all the necessities that the British people need. Makes you wonder what the Royal Navy is up to."

In Teddy's mind, the images were still vivid of ships burning in the night and bodies floating on dark water, of Morgan giving him his life jacket. He knew very well what the Royal navy was "up to." But he couldn't say anything about that to Mel. He was about to put a spoonful of oatmeal into his mouth, when another thought made him hesitate.

"The man I'm replacing," he said. "Captain Bidwell said he's sick from food poisoning."

Mel had just shoved a forkful of powdered eggs into his mouth. He looked up from his plate and saw Teddy with his spoon halfway between his bowl and his mouth. Mel swallowed and then laughed.

"Poor ol' Danny boy didn't get sick from eating 'ere," he said. "It was a bad lot of bangers an' mash 'e ate in a pub in town what brought 'im to grief. Watch out for the pub food when you're about town on leave. With everything in short supply, flippin' publicans will stuff the sausages with anything, even if it barks or says meow. Blimey! Do you think the nasty little germs that cause food poisoning could live in *this*?"

Mel held up a forkful of powdered eggs as though to show Teddy what a hostile habitat it would be for any organisms dangerous to humans. Then he slid the lump off the fork and into his mouth.

"Mmm! Loverly!" he said

Teddy ate his oatmeal. It was like paste, and he needed a mouthful of tea to wash it down. The tea was weak, and Teddy wished he'd put a bit of milk in it as Mel had done. Then he tried the powdered eggs. He wasn't sure what word he'd have used if his mother had served them to him for breakfast, but it certainly wouldn't have been "loverly."

As they were eating, Teddy heard the sound of another approaching aircraft. It quickly became *very* loud and then thunderous. The whole building seemed to shake as the plane roared overhead. Teddy fought an urge to duck under the table for cover.

"*That* wasn't another Spitfire!" he said as the din died away.

"Sounds like you're learnin', me ol' *Caniedian* mate," Mel said. "Every type of plane, British or German, 'as its own song, just like the little birdies. Any bloke sittin' in 'ere can tell you without lookin' that was a Lanc."

"Lanc?" Teddy said.

"Lancaster bomber," Mel replied. "You and me will be in one tonight, droppin' a few little presents on the Nazis."

Tonight! Captain Bidwell had told Teddy that his name was on that night's Battle Order. The cold reality struck Teddy that he was going to be on an actual bombing raid, in a plane the enemy would be trying to destroy. Why should *he* be in yet another terrible situation? He'd already been in the nightmare of no man's land, had seen Joe die and had known the darkness of blindness. He'd had a ship torpedoed from under him, and he had felt the soul-deep terror and despair of drifting like a speck on the sea. What more could the weirdness possibly want of him?

The old veteran had said that his situation had to be desperate for him to use the poem. In War Games strategy, a good player looked two or three moves ahead. Teddy didn't have to look very far ahead to know that once he was in the air over enemy territory, he'd be in a desperate situation.

Teddy was thinking about the next lines of the poem, wondering if this was the right moment to say them, when four young men entered the room. They deposited some cricket equipment on a bench inside the door and then headed straight for Mel and Teddy's table. Mel stood to attention and saluted, so Teddy did the same. He saw that the man in the lead, who appeared to be a little older than the others, had an officer's stripes on his sleeve.

"At ease," the officer said. "Well, Lynne, are you going to introduce us?"

"Yes, sir!" Mel said. "Lieutenant King, this is Gunner Ted Nugent, from Canada."

Teddy noticed that Mel pronounced King's rank as "*Left*-enant."

"From Canada, are you?" Lieutenant King said, giving Teddy a good look up and down.

"Yes, sir," Teddy replied.

"Can't say I've been all that impressed with some of you fellows from across the pond that I've met, Nugent. They lack discipline. Do you know what the Londoners of Sergeant Lynne's class say about you Canadians?"

Teddy thought he saw Mel flinch just a little when the lieutenant said "Sergeant Lynne's *class*."

"No, sir, I don't," said Teddy.

Lieutenant King had an accent that to Teddy's ears sounded like the aristocratic English characters he'd seen in movies. But to Teddy's surprise, and Mel's obvious discomfort, the officer's response sounded like he was mocking Mel's Cockney accent.

"Well, they *compline* that you *Caniedians* are over*pied* and over 'ere. What do you think of that, Nugent?"

Teddy noticed one of the men behind the lieutenant wink at him and give his head a little shake.

"I'm afraid I don't know anything about that, sir. I've only just arrived here," Teddy replied.

"Well, you'd better be up to the job, Nugent," Lieutenant King said. "You won't be shooting at ducks or geese or owls or whatever flying things you Canadians blast away at for Sunday dinner."

"I'll do my best, sir," Teddy said.

"That's hardly reassuring," the lieutenant responded. Then he told the others, "Air test in one hour, men. Be punctual.

Lynne, make sure your pet colonial doesn't wander off looking for a jamboree camp. I suspect from the salute he just gave me that he thinks he's in the Boy Scouts."

Teddy felt his face flush with embarrassment as Lieutenant King left. It wasn't so much because the officer had tried to humiliate him but because in his nervousness he'd forgotten the proper salute Mel had shown him.

Mel must have seen the crimson in Teddy's face. "No need to weep an' wail over 'im, mate," Mel said when the lieutenant was gone. "I don't, and 'e 'as it in for me all the time."

"I don't think he likes me," Teddy said.

"You mustn't take it personally, old boy," said the man who had winked at Teddy. "Bertie doesn't like anybody not to the manor born, as they say. To put it bluntly, he's a snob."

"His name is *Bertie*?" Teddy asked. Somehow the name didn't suit the man.

"Lieutenant Albert Edward King, our flight engineer and Captain Bidwell's co-pilot," the man explained. "Like so many other unsuspecting English lads of his breeding, he was named after royalty. In his case, his late Majesty King Edward the Seventh. Bertie is a King who was named for a king. Get it? And he's a lieutenant who has his nose out of joint because he's not a captain. My name, by the way, is Henry. Not after Henry the Eighth. I'm just Henry Platt, the bomber's navigator. Pleased to meet you, Nugent."

Platt held out his hand and Teddy shook it. Mel introduced him to the other two members of the crew, bomb-aimer Martin Halliday and rear gunner David Jones.

"Don't you dare call me Tail-Gunner Charlie," Jones said. "That's a Yank term. Very un-British. Glad to meet you, Nugent."

The men pulled up chairs and sat around the table.

"I suppose Lynne has been giving you his usual bit about you shooting at the Nazi planes he misses," Jones said. "Don't pay attention to his malarkey. He hasn't shot down anything yet."

"Don't listen to this bloke," Mel said. "All 'e does is sit back nice and cozy-like in 'is glass blister at the tail, 'avin' a nice cuppa while lads like you and me deal with the Jerry buzzards."

Teddy could tell they were kidding each other. He said, "Actually, we saw you playing cricket, and Sergeant Lynne was explaining to me that it's a more civilized game than Canadian hockey."

"My word!" said Halliday. "That sounds like something dear old Bertie would say."

"Oh, I was just 'avin' 'im on," said Mel. "Ted's an alright bloke."

"Do you guys always play cricket before . . . taking off?" Teddy asked. He thought it an odd way to prepare for a dangerous mission.

"Not always," said Platt. "Sometimes we play football or rugby."

"If it's raining, we'll sit in here and play cards," said Jones. "Anything to pass the time and keep your mind off the night ahead."

"Like Drake playing a game of bowls before sailing out to fight the Armada," said Platt.

"And then he played cannon-bowls," Halliday said, and the others groaned.

The night ahead! Teddy was very apprehensive about what the coming hours would bring. He had no idea what it would be like to be in a plane flying above enemy territory. These men had all done it before, and he wanted to ask them questions. He just didn't know how to start without revealing he knew nothing about the job he was expected to do and that he was scared. After thinking about it for a few moments, he asked "So, where are we going tonight?"

"Don't know," Mel said. "They never tell us the target until briefing. Until then, it's all a big secret. Very 'ush, 'ush."

Then Platt asked, "Is this your first combat mission, Ted?"

Teddy glanced around the table at the faces looking back at him. "Yes," he replied quietly. "I'm afraid it is."

"What you mean, mate, is that you're *afraid*. End of story," said Mel. "Right?"

"Right," Teddy replied even more quietly, not wanting anyone beyond this circle of new companions to hear him.

"Well, we've all been there, mate. First time and all that, 'aven't we, lads?" Mel said.

The others all said yes, with knowing nods and raised eyebrows.

"I recall Bertie's first mission," said Platt. "He threw up in the cockpit. Ghastly business! On my first mission I had the decency to throw up before boarding the aircraft. Oh, and a bit of advice for you, Ted. Visit the loo before boarding."

The other men laughed. Mel said, "Look, mate, all you 'ave to do is look to your own job. Biddy and Bertie fly the plane. Platt guides us to the target. 'alliday lets the bombs go so they 'it the target. I look after the wireless and the front turret. Jones sits on 'is fanny in the rear turret. Your job, and nothing else, is to keep a sharp eye in the dorsal turret and shoot at any bloody plane that ain't one of ours."

"Jerry will throw a lot of anti-aircraft fire at us," Jones said. "We lads in the gun turrets have front row seats when the flak starts popping all around. It looks scary, Ted. But don't pay it too much mind. It's mostly fireworks. And don't forget, that blister you're sitting in is made of glass thick enough to stop bullets. I've had mine pockmarked a few times, and not a scratch on me."

"Wet 'is drawers, though," Mel said.

The others laughed.

"Not as bad as what you done in yours, mate," Jones replied, and they laughed again.

"That's why it's a good idea to make that visit to the loo," said Platt, to more laughter.

Now Teddy understood that the "loo" was the toilet. And he had the feeling that all the joking and laughter was a front to cover up a shared fear.

"What did Bertie . . . I mean, Lieutenant King mean about an air test?" Teddy asked.

"Before a plane is cleared for a mission, the ground crew

goes over it from nose to tail," Halliday said. "They repair any damage it might have received on its previous flight and make sure everything is in top working order before it goes up again. You know, put on that extra little dab of glue so the wings don't fall off. That sort of thing."

"*Glue?*" said Teddy.

"Oh, 'e's 'avin' you on," Mel laughed. "When the ground crew is done, we take the Lanc up for a little air test. Just ten or fifteen minutes to make sure there's no bugs in the works. Sometimes Biddy tells the ground crew to come along for the ride. That's 'is way of keeping 'em on their toes; make sure they do their job right."

Teddy was relieved to hear that Captain Bidwell took such measures on behalf of his crew. He'd met the captain only briefly and wished he knew more about the man who was his great-grandfather. He asked, "Is Captain Bidwell anything like Lieutenant King?"

"Oh, blimey, no!" exclaimed Mel. "Different as night and day, they are. Bertie knows 'is job well enough. But . . . well, I'll put it this way. If the plane was going down, and we was short a parachute, between the two of them, Biddy would be the bloke to give 'is chute to another man."

"Oh, come now, Lynne," said Platt. "Bertie would give his parachute to another man . . . after first making sure he had a good hold on Biddy."

Within the hour, Teddy and the rest of the crew were walking across the airfield. He was surprised to see that it actually was a *field*. Just a flat grassy area with many places where it appeared holes had been filled in with dirt. Mel noticed him looking at them and said, "Bomb craters from air raids. Jerry 'ad us scurryin', 'e did, before 'itler decided to bomb London instead. We lost some good mates."

The field was alive with activity as ground crews went about their duties. Teddy could see that some of them were working on the planes, like the mechanics he'd seen when he went with his father to take the car to a repair shop. But others weren't servicing the engines. They were removing parts, even whole wings, that had bullet holes and scorch marks. Teddy did not at all like the idea of flying in a patched-up plane.

The air vibrated with the hum of engines. The smell of fuel was everywhere. Teddy saw three Hurricane fighter planes roar down the packed-earth runway and take off, one after the other. He asked about the fire engine and ambulance he spotted parked near the edge of the field.

"Just in case," Halliday said.

Teddy was about to ask, "In case of what?" But he already knew the answer.

As they made their way through the clusters of aircraft, Platt identified the different types of bombers. "That's a Halifax," he said, pointing at one. "Those two over there are Wellingtons. That one is a Hampden. But most of these beauties are Lancasters. Better than anything the Nazis have, if you ask me."

Teddy's group had to get out of the way of a small truck hauling a trailer that was loaded with bombs. They looked like the artillery shells Teddy had already seen, but bigger. He thought there was something sinister about them, that they were sleeping monsters just waiting to be awakened.

"Are those going into our plane?" he asked.

"Not until after the air test," Halliday replied. "Once we've had our little whirl, the armourers will load us up."

"And then we'll be dropping them on —"

Teddy had been about to say "people," but Platt interrupted. "The enemy! That's what you have to keep in mind, Ted. You Canadian chaps weren't here when the blitz started. We're just giving the Germans a taste of their own medicine. Too bloody bad if they don't like it!"

Teddy understood. At least, he told himself that he did. But he'd seen television news reports of bombing attacks in trouble spots all over the world. Once the sleeping monster was awakened in its explosive fury, it didn't pick and choose its victims. It killed or maimed every man, woman and child within reach of its destructive force. He had that queasy feeling in his stomach again.

"Well, there you all are. Almost a minute late. I suppose the Canadian kept you dawdling."

Lieutenant King stood beside their bomber, looking at his watch. The men saluted, and this time Teddy got it right.

"The crew is all present, sir," Mel said.

"Right, then!" said the lieutenant. "Captain Bidwell was

called to HQ, so I'll be taking us up for the test. Everybody get on board. And Nugent, don't test-fire your guns until we're over water. We have enough problem with the Jerries killing British civilians without you adding to their score."

Teddy knew better than to react to what Lieutenant King had said. His attention was focused on something else. He was looking over the huge, four-engine Lancaster bomber. He'd seen big passenger planes at airports and had flown in them on vacation trips. The Lanc was nothing like them. The airliners were sleek, usually white and silver, and propelled by jet engines. They were flying buses that carried people on business and holiday trips.

The Lanc, with its grey-and-green camouflage colouring, had a dark and menacing look to it — like a winged beast of prey. It looked as solid and heavy as an army tank. He wondered how the four propellers, big as they were, could lift such a massive machine off the ground and carry it through the air.

Test-fire your guns. Lieutenant King's words jolted Teddy, even though he ignored the intended insult. What was he going to do when he climbed into the turret? He had no idea how to operate the weapon.

The men boarded the plane and Lieutenant King went straight to the cockpit. Teddy was surprised at how cramped the crew's space was in such a big aircraft. Packed into a small area were the stations for the navigator, the bomb-aimer, and the person who operated the wireless — the plane's radio.

Each station had its own specialized equipment. Throughout the narrow interior of the fuselage were electrical cables and panels, gauges and instruments that were as alien to Teddy as the controls of Han Solo's *Millennium Falcon* in *Star Wars*. He saw ammunition boxes and a squat bucket-like object that Mel told him was an Elsan toilet. One look at it, and Teddy knew he'd follow Platt's advice about visiting the loo.

The plane was well-equipped with many things Teddy hoped the crew wouldn't have to use on that night's mission: first-aid kits and fire extinguishers, flare guns and an emergency axe, an inflatable rubber dinghy and — stowed in clearly-marked locations near each crew member's station — parachutes. The idea of jumping out of the plane with one of those things was terrifying to Teddy. He knew the other crew members had been trained in the use of their parachutes, but he'd never even seen one except in movies.

Lieutenant King taxied the bomber to the end of the runway. The engines made a terrific din and the plane shook as it hurtled forward, gathering speed. Then it was airborne.

Platt and Halliday sat down at their instruments. Jones headed for the tail area and disappeared into his turret. Mel sat at the wireless and quickly confirmed that it was in good working order. Then he got up to go to his turret in the bomber's nose. Teddy saw a solution to one of his problems.

Lieutenant King was occupied with flying the plane, and the other crew members were distracted by their duties. The noise from the engines was loud enough that Teddy could talk without being overheard if he kept his voice down.

"Say, Mel, I've never actually been in a nose turret," he said. "Mind if I have a look?"

"Not at all, mate." Mel replied. "Best view in the 'ouse."

Teddy followed Mel into the nose section and watched him climb into the glass blister. Looking over Mel's shoulder, he could see that the view was indeed more spectacular than anything he'd ever seen from the window of an airliner. He could see sky above, the horizon straight ahead and below, the fields of the English countryside — which suddenly gave way to the sea as the plane swept over the coastline.

"Loverly, ain't it?" Mel said as he prepared his guns for test-firing.

"It sure is," Teddy replied.

He watched closely, memorizing Mel's every move. The routine was similar to what Teddy had seen Morgan's gun crew do on the *Wolverine*. Then Mel fired a short burst. The racket was deafening, but Mel said, "Sounds loverly, don't it?"

"Do I have the same guns in my turret?" Teddy asked.

Mel looked around at him with a quizzical expression. "Are you asking me if you 'ave a pair of 303 Browning machine guns? Blimey, mate! Of course you do. What did you think? An American gangster Tommy gun? Better get to your turret now before Bertie wonders what we're up to."

Two minutes later, Teddy was sitting in the big glass blister that was the dorsal gun turret. Located on top of the bomber not quite midway between the nose and the tail, it gave Teddy a view of the sky above unobstructed by anything but clouds. He had a clear view in every direction except below. As a War Games player, he now understood the strategic placing of the gun turrets. Mel, in the nose turret, could see enemy fighter planes attacking from the front and below. Jones, in the tail turret, could see them coming from behind and below. In the dorsal turret, the gunner would see the German fighters swooping down from above.

Teddy hoped more than anything that that wouldn't happen. But he had to be ready if it did. Picturing in his mind each step Mel had taken, Teddy got his guns ready for action. Words he'd heard in movies popped into his head: *Locked and loaded!* Then he fired a burst — and couldn't make the guns stop!

Teddy was startled to find that the weapon jumped in his hands with every bullet the muzzles spat out. It was like trying to hold onto the motorized rototiller his father had once rented to make a new garden bed in the yard. The guns jerked this way and that, spraying bullets all over the sky. Teddy finally managed to get the weapon under control and stop the firing. He climbed out of the turret as quickly as he could. Mel, Halliday, Jones and Platt stood staring at him.

"Spot a flock of geese, did you, old boy?" Platt asked.

"Just some good old Canadian enthusiasm," Halliday said.

"Maybe our Ted thinks it's the Fourth of July," said Jones.

"That's American," Platt said.

Mel didn't say anything. He just gave Teddy a warning look and with a slight turn of his head, indicated the cockpit. Lieutenant King had heard the firing.

The air test lasted only fifteen minutes. When the plane was back on the ground and had come to a stop, Lieutenant King stormed out of the cockpit. He was livid.

"*NUGENT!*" he bellowed. "What in blazes was that?"

"I'm sorry, sir," Teddy said. "I was testing the guns and —"

"Never mind the excuses!" the lieutenant snapped. "I know you Canadians. No discipline! You think it's all a big game, don't you? No Jerry bombs are falling on Canada, so you think you can come over here and just play at war games! It's too late to have you replaced for tonight's mission, Nugent, but I'm putting you on report. I don't want you in my crew any longer than is absolutely necessary."

Turning his attention from Teddy, who was red-faced and wondering if now would be a good time to recite the next lines of the poem, Lieutenant King said, "Briefing at eigh-teen-hundred hours, men. Don't be late. Not even by a bloody minute! Now go and get some sleep."

Sleep! Teddy thought. *Sleep, dream, nightmare! Whatever it is, I wish I could wake up from it.*

Back in their hut, the men stretched out on their cots to rest before the long night. Mel's cot was next to Teddy's. During the walk from the bomber, after the scolding Lieu-tenant King had given him, Teddy had been silent. The other crew members had left him alone. But now Mel asked, "What 'appened in the turret, mate?"

"Didn't you hear what Lieutenant King said?" Teddy replied sullenly. "I'm an undisciplined Canadian. He's right. I shouldn't be here."

"Oh, 'e just likes to 'ear 'imself sound off," Mel said. "Besides, we ain't 'is crew. We're Captain Bidwell's. But me and the other lads would find it a comfort to know that you can 'andle them guns, Ted. Can you?"

"Yeah," Teddy said curtly. "I won't let the team down."

Then he closed his eyes, wishing that he'd doze off for at least a short nap. But he was very worried about the coming night. What if he *did* let the others down? Like Lieutenant King had said, this wasn't a game.

Despite his anxiety, Teddy drifted off. In his semi-dream he heard Paul say, "You're not a gunner, Ted. I'm not joking this time, buddy. This isn't War Games."

Then he heard Valerie. "You've got to tell the truth, Teddy. Those men are risking their lives. You know you're playing a game, but they aren't, and you have to stop now."

Teddy wanted to tell them both that it wasn't him playing the game. It was the weirdness that had put him in this place and this time. He wanted to get out of it, but that wasn't up to him. He had no choice but to go along until his situation was . . . desperate.

But Teddy knew in his half-slumber that the voices in his head weren't really those of Paul and Valerie. They were his own mind's invention, a means of arguing with himself. Although he wasn't really a gunner, he felt he could handle the weapon now that he'd had that unexpected surprise in the turret. What good would it do to tell the others that had been the very first time he'd ever been in a gun turret? The lieutenant had said that it was too late to replace him. The other crew members would be risking their lives whether he was in the turret or not. Teddy believed he *had* to be there.

Late in the afternoon, Teddy was jarred from his fitful sleep when Platt called out, "Wakey-wakey, chaps. Duty calls."

As Teddy got up from his cot, he noticed Mel take something out of his locker and stuff it into his pocket. He asked what it was.

"An old Queen Victoria penny that me dad gave me when I was a little 'un," Mel said. "You know, for luck."

"You carry a good luck piece?" Teddy asked. He'd never believed in such things.

"Just about everybody does," Mel replied. "Can't 'urt, can it? Jones 'as a St. Christopher medal. Catholic, 'e is. 'Alliday is from Kent. 'E keeps a little stone 'e picked up on the beach there in 'is pocket. Platt 'as a pocket watch 'is granddad carried all through the Boer War. Figures if it kept the ol' bloke alive through that bit of fuss an' bother, it should work for 'im in this one. Ain't you got something to bring you a little 'elp from Lady Luck?"

Teddy thought for a moment and then said, "Yes, I do. I have a lucky poem."

Mel gave Teddy an odd look. "A poem?" he said. "You mean like from Shakespeare or Dickens or one of them blokes?"

"No," Teddy replied. "It's by a Canadian poet."

"You got it on you?" Mel asked. "I've never read no Canadian poem. Let's 'ave a look."

Teddy said, "Can't. It's in my head."

The men walked to the canteen and sat down to their pre-flight supper. Teddy wasn't surprised to see a slice of bread and a small portion of the notorious mutton on his plate. But there was an ample helping of a side dish that drew an exclamation from Mel.

"Beans!" he cried. "Again! Blimey! As if we don't 'ave enough bloody explosives on the bloody plane!"

The men laughed, but after that they ate their meal quietly. There was none of the joking and bantering Teddy had heard earlier. The serious business of war was drawing too close.

The men finished their supper. When they stood up to go, each one knocked twice on the table. Teddy did, too. As they were leaving the canteen, he asked Mel why they'd done that.

"Knock on wood for luck," Mel said. "So it won't be our last meal together."

Mel's answer gave Teddy a chill. "Do you really believe all that good luck stuff works?" he asked.

"Well, it 'as so far," Mel said.

They paid a visit to the latrine and then went to the base headquarters for briefing. Captain Bidwell and Lieutenant King were already there. Teddy saw the lieutenant look at his watch. He didn't say a word, which Teddy guessed meant that they were right on time. He wondered if Lieutenant King had said anything to Captain Bidwell about him.

Teddy and his group joined other bomber crews sitting in

a large room that had a small raised platform at the front. Mel, Platt and the others exchanged greetings with fellow airmen. Teddy heard snatches of conversations mostly concerning what that night's target would be. Hamburg? Cologne? Berlin? He heard a man say, "Wherever Adolf is would suit me."

Someone else said, "Never mind Adolf. I'd like to drop one on the blighter that stole the new underwear me mum sent me."

The chatter stopped when an officer stepped onto the platform and called for attention.

"That's Major Ash," Mel whispered to Teddy. "The base commander."

When the room had quieted down and he knew he had the men's eyes and ears, Major Ash said, "Gentlemen, tonight we're going to help our lads in the Royal Navy and hit the Nazis hard in a place that will hurt them the most."

Mel whispered to Teddy again. "Right-oh! Below the belt. Sounds good to me."

Lieutenant King gave Mel an angry look and put a finger to his lips. Mel sat back, feigning innocence. Teddy heard him say, "Twit!" under his breath.

Major Ash continued. "Tonight, we're going to bomb the U-boat yards in Boulogne. As I speak, your planes are being loaded with blockbusters that will crack those concrete pens wide open."

The room erupted with cheers. The airmen shook hands

all around and patted each other on the back. Teddy knew why they were celebrating. The U-boats were strangling Britain. If the RAF could destroy their bases, there would be fewer wolf packs to attack the convoys. After his experiences with A.J., Commander Steele, Lieutenant Gordon and other men of the *Wolverine*, Teddy didn't feel quite so guilty about participating in a bombing raid.

Major Ash again called for quiet. Then he pulled down a big map that hung on the wall at the back of the platform. It showed southern England and a large part of France. The city of Boulogne was circled in red. A black line traced the route the bomber force would take to the target and then back to England. As much of the flight path as possible would be over water to reduce exposure to enemy ground-based anti-aircraft fire.

A Military Intelligence officer stepped onto the platform. He showed projected photographic images taken by RAF reconnaissance planes of the U-boat yards and nearby landmarks. Not all would be clearly visible from the air at night, but specially equipped pathfinder planes flying ahead of the bombers would locate the targets and mark them with flares to guide the bomb-aimers. The officer told the men everything Military Intelligence knew of German defences in that area: anti-aircraft balloons, anti-aircraft guns, searchlights and the proximity of Luftwaffe bases for Junkers JU 88s and Messerschmitt ME 110s, the Germans' most dreaded night-fighters.

A meteorologist explained what kind of weather the attack force could expect. Cloud cover was heavy over the French coast. That was good, because the bombers would fly above it, hidden from enemy anti-aircraft gunners below. But over Boulogne, where the planes would have to fly at a lower altitude for their bombing runs, the cloud cover was thin, and the light of a three-quarters moon would make them visible and vulnerable.

Mel told Teddy behind his hand in a hushed voice, "Before the war, I never thought I'd 'ate the bloody moon."

Lieutenant King shot Mel another impatient look.

An RAF navigation specialist mounted the platform next. What he had to say was strictly for Platt and his colleagues, so Teddy sat back and looked around the room. He saw that some of the men — who he guessed were not navigators — were writing on small note pads. He nudged Mel and asked what they were doing.

"Last letters 'ome — maybe," Mel said. "They'll give 'em to the CO, just in case. If a bloke comes back safe and sound, 'e'll get it back. But if 'e buys it, the major will make sure it gets delivered."

"Buys it?" Teddy said.

"Gets killed," Mel replied.

The specialist distributed bundles of maps and charts to all of the navigators. Major Ash said, "Good luck, gentlemen, and Godspeed." With that, the briefing session was over.

The men filed out of the room and went next door to the

flight office, where they lined up to receive their gear for the night's mission. Teddy was given an airman's helmet, goggles, gloves, an oxygen mask, first-aid kit, battle-dress overalls and a sheepskin-lined leather bomber jacket.

Should he have to bail out over occupied territory, Teddy had an escape kit that contained matches, chewing gum, high-energy candy, fishing line, a compass, a sewing needle and thread, soap and a razor, a soft plastic water bottle and water purification tablets. He also had an escape purse with maps, French currency, a card with a list of phrases in English and French and a tiny hacksaw blade. The kit and the purse were both compact enough to fit into a pocket of his jacket or trousers. In addition, maps were sewn into the collar of his jacket, and some of its buttons were compasses.

Each man had to empty his pockets of all personal effects including wallets, photographs, letters and good luck pieces. It all went into brown envelopes and would be given back to the owners upon their return. If a man didn't come back, his property would be sent to his family. Teddy saw Mel give his Queen Victoria penny a few rubs between his thumb and finger before dropping it into the envelope. He felt a twinge of guilt that he could keep his good luck poem because it was in his head.

When the men were properly equipped, they climbed into the backs of trucks Mel called lorries to be driven to their bombers.

"Nice of them to give us a ride," Teddy joked.

"They ain't doing this out of the goodness of their 'earts," Mel said. "What we just 'eard at the briefing was for nobody's ears but ours. They 'ave to be sure nobody talks to nobody they shouldn't talk to before we're on our planes. Never know where Nazi spies might be lurkin' about."

Teddy found it hard to believe that spies could be on the air base or that any of the men in the crews would pass on information that might be useful to the enemy. But the atmosphere of secrecy that had enveloped the base with nightfall told him that the officers in charge were taking every precaution.

The airfield was in darkness so that no activity could be seen from beyond the base perimeter or from the air. The windows of all the buildings were blacked out. The lorry drivers had to find their way without the use of headlights.

The lorry in which Teddy and his crewmates were riding stopped at their Lanc. When Teddy got out, he could see that some of the bombers were already taxiing toward the runway, guided by men with flashlights. But there was no disguising the rumble of accelerating engines and the roar of bombers taking off. Teddy saw the first one leave the ground like a shadowy phantom and then disappear into the cloudy night sky.

To Teddy's surprise, before boarding the Lanc, his crewmates all went to the rear wheel and peed on it.

"For luck," Mel explained.

Teddy thought they depended an awful lot on luck. Nonetheless, he contributed to the ritual.

Minutes later, Teddy's plane was hurtling down the runway. This time, it was loaded with bombs and carried the weight of enough fuel to keep it in the air for a long distance and longer hours. Teddy thought he could actually sense the bomber's heaviness as the engines struggled to lift it off the ground.

Then they were airborne. Mel, Halliday and Platt went directly to their stations. Lieutenant King, as flight engineer, gave his attention to a panel of dials and gauges to the rear of the co-pilot's seat. Teddy thought that he and Jones wouldn't be needed in their turrets until the plane was over enemy territory. But he was sitting on the rest-bed when Jones told him, "Don't get too comfortable there, mate. We have to get to our guns. No telling when we'll run into Jerry bandits."

The plane was still climbing, so Teddy had to hold on tight to his seat. He felt the aircraft level off as it reached cruising altitude. Then, before he could go to his turret, Captain Bidwell turned the controls over to Lieutenant King. He climbed out of his seat in the cockpit and stepped back into the crew's cabin. In his hand he had a brown paper bag from which he took peeled hard-boiled eggs and raw carrot-sticks.

"Thought you lads might like a little something for the long flight," he said as he passed them around. "Sorry there's no salt and pepper, but we must make do, mustn't we. Be sure to eat those carrots, men. Best thing for your night vision. How are you doing there, Nugent? Ready to show the Nazis the kind of stuff you Canadian lads are made of?"

"Yes, sir," Teddy replied, wishing he could say more to this man. If only he could tell Captain Bidwell how closely related they were.

The captain returned to the cockpit. With a hard-boiled egg and a few carrot sticks in his pocket, Teddy headed for his turret. As he passed the wireless operator's station, he heard Mel grumble, "Blimey! Beans and 'ard-boiled eggs. Now there's an explosive combination for lads in a closed space! Where's me flippin' parachute?"

It was cold at that altitude, and the interior of the plane wasn't heated. Perched in his glass blister atop the aircraft, Teddy was glad he'd taken Captain Bidwell's advice and worn the woollen sweater he'd called a jumper. He munched on a carrot stick and wondered if it really would improve his night vision.

Teddy recalled what Mel had said about his front turret having the best view. He wasn't sure if that was true, because from where he sat the view was spectacular. Because the plane was flying above the clouds, Teddy could see the night sky as he had never seen it before. The stars in their thousands twinkled in the infinite blackness. Within just a quarter of an hour, Teddy caught sight of the trails of more shooting stars than he'd ever seen in his life. He'd never seen the face of the moon — at least the three-quarters of it that was visible — so stark in white and shadow. Moonlight shining on the top of the cloud layer made it look like the surface of some land in a fantasy tale. Occasionally, Teddy saw flashes in a distant cloud bank. He knew from science class in school that the shooting stars were actually tiny meteorites burning up in the earth's atmosphere, and the flashes in the clouds were caused by electrical storms.

Teddy also saw the forms of some of the other bombers. Their dark colouring absorbed the moonlight, so they didn't shine. But they were silhouetted against the reflected light of the sea of clouds, and as they passed any given part of the sky, they momentarily blotted out the stars, like dragons sweeping across the heavens.

Teddy watched for German "bandits." On the *Wolverine*, he'd feared an enemy that hid in the dark waters below. He'd scanned the surface of the ocean for sign of a periscope. Here in his turret on the Lanc, he was afraid of an enemy that could be anywhere, that could come from any direction. And when that foe appeared, it would be a fighter plane with guns blazing. Captain Bidwell and the others were counting on him to do his part in protecting the plane. "*Can I do it?*" he asked himself. "*What if I can't?*" He didn't want to think about that.

The night sky, for all its marvels, became a threat — a thing of terror. Teddy forgot about the boiled egg in his pocket but devoured the carrot sticks, hoping that if they really worked, they'd work fast. In spite of his layers of warm clothing, Teddy shivered as he peered into the dark and menacing sky.

As time passed, Teddy realized that his station in the dorsal turret was a lonely place. He was cut off from the company of the crew in the cockpit and cabin below. From time to time, he'd hear Captain Bidwell's voice in his headphones.

"Gunner Nugent! Keeping awake up there, lad?"

"Yes, sir," Teddy would reply. "Wide awake, sir."

"Good show, lad. Stay sharp."

But as much as Teddy tried to focus on his job, distracting thoughts crept into his mind. He tried to shake them away. But they were persistent.

He was in this plane because of some trick of the weirdness. All of the other men, even Lieutenant King, as unlikeable as he was, had voluntarily placed themselves in great danger. They didn't have his "lucky poem." Neither had Tom and Joe, or the men of the *Wolverine*. None of them had fallen asleep in a warm and comfortable bed and awakened in a strange time and place. They had chosen to lay their lives on the line. *He* was the stranger in *their* worlds and a reluctant visitor at that.

It seemed to Teddy that more than a lifetime had passed since the most important thing in the world to him was skipping a Remembrance Day ceremony so he could play in a War Games competition. He was no longer even sure why that had meant so much to him. If he didn't play, it wouldn't be — as Valerie would put it — "the end of the world." But for the other men in the plane, indeed, all of the men in all of the planes and in the trenches and on the ships, the end of the world for them was a frightening possibility. One that had come true for Joe and Morgan and so many others.

Teddy had all of the lines of the poem fixed in his mind. If his situation became desperate enough, he had a way out. But he felt that he was a coward. The others wouldn't have that opportunity to escape.

Deep in Teddy's mind, beneath all the thoughts that tumbled through his head as he watched for German night-fighters, was one stark, nagging, guilt-ridden fear. What if something happened to silence him before he could say the next lines of the poem? Would he wake up again in his own bed, *ever*?

"Target dead ahead! Look alive, lads!"

At the sound of Captain Bidwell's voice, Teddy braced himself for whatever was to come. His heart hammered in his chest and his mouth went dry. He felt pressure on his body as the plane made a sudden, steep descent for its bombing run. Looking down the Lanc toward the nose, he could see other bombers swooping toward the target area.

The city of Boulogne was in blackout, but marker flares dropped by the pathfinders were falling on the waterfront where the U-boat pens were located. The moonlight revealed zeppelin-shaped anti-aircraft balloons, anchored to the ground by cables that were deadly snares for planes. The same light that enabled the bomber pilots to avoid the balloons also made their planes visible to German gunners on the ground.

Teddy suddenly found himself in the midst of a terrifying chaos. The beams of dozens of searchlights pierced the night sky, shooting up like tentacles in search of victims. They criss-crossed each other in what looked to Teddy like a grotesque dance of light. Flack from anti-aircraft guns burst all around him, filling the air with fire, smoke and a continuous crackle of bursting shells. It was as though a fireworks factory had been set ablaze, throwing all of its fury into the sky.

Bigger explosions erupted on the ground as the first bombs hit. Teddy saw the geysers of flame that bloomed in hellish patterns, making the world below look like a garden of fire. The sound of the explosions was delayed by distance and muffled by his turret's thick glass and his helmet. But he could distinguish it from the racket of the flack. It hit his ears like the muted thuds he'd heard in Joe and Tom's dugout. Teddy told himself that he wouldn't want to be down there.

"We've got bandits!" This time it was Mel's voice Teddy heard. "Above and be-'ind, and closing in fast!"

Teddy swung his turret around and looked up, but he couldn't see anything. Then there was a flash in the darkness that wasn't made by flack. An engine on one of the bombers had been hit by fighter fire and burst into flames.

Teddy heard the high-pitched scream of the night-fighters before he caught a glimpse of one. It sliced through the searchlight beams like a nighthawk diving on prey, and then it was gone from sight. The flames of the stricken bomber became an inferno as it exploded.

Then the night-fighters were everywhere, like a horde of devils. In the darkness, Teddy saw flashes of gunfire from the battle between the fighters and the bombers' gunners. Flaming aircraft fell to the earth like spent Roman candles. Teddy couldn't tell if they were German or British. He swung his guns back and forth looking for something to shoot at. But the night-fighters were fast and elusive. Every time he thought he had one in his sights, it was gone before he could fire. There was a moment when his hesitation was fortunate. In the wild confusion, he'd almost opened fire on a Lanc.

Teddy heard Jones report to Captain Bidwell that a fighter was coming at them from behind. He felt the plane swerve as the captain took evasive action, and heard the rapid fire of Jones's guns. Teddy looked toward the tail and saw the underside of the fighter as it swooped up to escape the stream of bullets. Teddy saw his chance and fired a burst. But shooting at one moving object from another was difficult, and he knew he'd missed.

In spite of being under attack, Captain Bidwell had to press on and complete the mission. The Lanc was now moving directly forward at the lowest altitude he dared take it, exposed to fire from the ground and above. The night was aglow from the fires burning throughout the Boulogne waterfront. Teddy heard Halliday announce, "Bombs away!" He knew that the Lanc had dropped its contribution to the destruction below. Now Captain Bidwell had to get his plane and crew home.

There was no let-up in the night-fighter attack. Teddy had tried to banish War Games from his mind, but he couldn't help thinking that if he were the German commander, he'd get every night-fighter in the air that he could and harass the bomber squadron all along its route home. He'd want to shoot down as many of them as possible, because every destroyed bomber was one that would never come back. The thought that this awful flight wasn't over meant that the terror wasn't, either. The running air battle that followed the bombing raid proved that Teddy's War Games tactic of putting yourself in the enemy's head had been correct. The way home was through a gauntlet.

Teddy thought that without the weight of the bombs and half of its fuel, the Lanc flew faster. But it still wasn't equal to the speed of the night-fighters. They buzzed through the bomber formation like falcons attacking a flock of lumbering geese. Their guns spat fire, and the bombers' gunners answered. More planes spiralled down in flames. In the moonlight, Teddy caught glimpses of white parachutes.

"Mission accomplished, lads," Captain Bidwell announced. "We're homeward bound. If you gunners can keep the Nazi blighters off our backs until we're over the sea, we'll soon be out of their range."

No sooner had the captain spoken than Teddy heard Jones shout, "Bandit! Coming right at me!"

Mel, now manning the guns in the nose turret, immediately cried, "Two bandits ahead, coming up from below!"

The racket from the nose and tail guns filled Teddy's ears as he twisted this way and that, trying to catch sight of the attackers. When he saw a German plane, it was only because it had been hit and was streaming red, yellow and blue flames. Then something struck the glass in front of his face with a loud *CRACK*! He instinctively shut his eyes and ducked as a night-fighter zoomed by just a few metres over his head. Teddy realized to his horror that a swarm of fighters was attacking the Lanc.

A bullet had struck the blister of Teddy's turret. It hadn't pierced the thick glass but had gouged out a fist-sized chunk. Teddy wondered how many such hits the glass could withstand before it disintegrated. At the same time, he knew it didn't matter how well the glass stood up to machine gun bullets if the plane went down.

Teddy felt panic taking hold of him and he tried to fight it. He fired a burst from his guns at nothing. He knew from the jumble of voices coming through his headphones that the plane was being riddled. Another night-fighter buzzed past in a diving attack, and an engine on one of the Lanc's wings burst into flames.

Teddy fired his guns again, and once more hit nothing.

Teddy was angry with himself. *I shouldn't be here*, he thought. *Lieutenant King was right! I'm useless! I'm not helping at all. These guys need a real gunner up here, not me. If I weren't here, Captain Bidwell might have sent somebody up here who knows what he's doing.*

The Lanc was shaking. Teddy thought the best thing he could do for his crewmates — and himself — was to say the rest of the poem. He was about to do that when he heard Mel cry, "Captain! I'm 'it, sir!"

A moment later, another engine was on fire. The Lanc was finished.

In a remarkably calm voice, Captain Bidwell said, "Bail out, lads."

Then he added, "That's an order, lads. GET OUT NOW!"

Teddy forgot about the poem. He climbed down from his turret and found the cabin in a shambles. Cannon fire from fighters had blasted holes in the fuselage and destroyed the wireless and other equipment. A fire was burning in the tail section, and a discarded extinguisher among the wreckage was evidence of a failed attempt to put it out.

Captain Bidwell was still in the pilot's seat, fighting to keep the doomed plane from losing altitude as long as possible. Lieutenant King was in the co-pilot's seat, trying to assist the captain.

"I gave you an order, Lieutenant," Captain Bidwell said, with just a hint of urgency in his voice.

"You have to get out, too, sir," Lieutenant King replied anxiously.

"I will as soon as the rest of you are out," said Captain Bidwell. "Now GO!"

The lieutenant clambered over his seat and joined the other men who were harnessing themselves into parachutes. Teddy saw that two of the crew were missing.

"Where are the others?" he cried.

"Jones is dead," Lieutenant King said. "Lynne was hit. If he were still alive, he'd be out here."

"He might need help!" Teddy said. He pushed his way past the others and headed for the nose turret.

"You can't help him, Nugent!" Lieutenant King shouted. "There isn't time. Obey orders and bail out!"

Teddy ignored him. The plane was rocking like a boat on rough water. Smoke filled the cabin. Teddy stumbled and then crawled forward into the nose section. He didn't look back to see if anyone followed. He heard Captain Bidwell cry, "OUT! OUT! OUT!" But he didn't know if the other crewmen were still there or if they'd jumped through the escape hatch.

Teddy reached the turret and tried to squeeze into the cramped space. Wind shrieked in through a saucer-sized hole in the glass blister. Mel was slumped over his guns. There was blood on his bomber jacket.

"Come on, Mel," Teddy urged. "You've got to get out."

There was no response. Teddy feared the worst, but he grabbed Mel's arm and shook it. He heard Mel groan.

"Come on, Mel, wake up!" Teddy pleaded.

Mel moaned and said weakly, "Blimey! If it ain't ol' Canada. Better get out, mate. Cheerio." Then he passed out again.

Teddy tried to pull Mel out of the turret, but he was limp and heavy. It was difficult to move him in the confined space. Teddy looked through the glass. In the moonlight, he could see the rippled surface of the sea below. It seemed to be coming up toward him, fast!

A last second, desperate hope struck Teddy. He wrapped his arms around Mel and quickly said, "Take up our quarrel with the foe: to you from failing hands we throw the torch; be yours to hold it high. If ye break faith with us who die . . ."

The Lanc hit the water.

5
Home Again

❀

"HANG ON, MEL. I'll get you out," Teddy murmured. "Just hang on."

He felt himself tossed in a maelstrom of darkness and floating lights. He panicked when he realized he no longer had a hold on Mel. Where was he? Had they escaped from the plane? What about Captain Bidwell and the rest of the crew? Were they all dead, like poor Jones?

Then Teddy woke up.

It was dark, and for a few moments Teddy was disoriented. He wondered what war the weirdness had put him into this time. Korea? The Middle East? Was he waking up in a barrack? A tent? A POW camp? Should he get up before some officer came and rousted him out of bed?

Then he realized he was in his own bed. To be sure, he pressed his fingers into the mattress he lay on and squeezed a handful of the blanket that covered him. They weren't coarse or damp, and they weren't smelly. They were definitely his. Teddy ran his hands down the side of his body. He was wearing his pajamas. He rubbed his bare feet together. He scratched his head and felt his face. His eyes and cheeks were wet, as though he'd been crying.

Teddy's vision adjusted to the dim light that snuck through a sliver of space between the curtains that were closed over the window. He could make out the familiar forms of things in his room: his desk, his bureau, the lamp on his bedside table. Almost afraid that the weirdness would play another trick on him, he reached out and switched on the lamp. As it clicked, he shut his eyes and counted to ten before opening them. The light made him blink, and for a moment he was afraid he'd hear the thud of artillery. But there was no sound, and all he could see was what he saw when he woke up every morning. The only difference was the poppy pinned to his pillow.

The clock on his bedside table said 6:15 a.m. The date in the bottom right corner was November 11. Only a few hours had passed since he'd fallen asleep, but he remembered things that had happened to him over . . . how much time? He didn't know. Except that he could recall minute by minute the time he'd spent with Tom and Joe, A.J. and Mel; it all added up to more than a few hours on the clock. It didn't seem possible that a sleeping brain could cram so much into such a short period.

The one thing Teddy was sure of, now that he was in his own bed at last, was that he didn't have to get up for another hour. He switched off the lamp, hoping to doze off again and not have such disturbing dreams. For some reason, he felt as tired as if he hadn't slept at all. And somewhere in the back of his mind, a voice told him that he hadn't been dreaming.

"*That's stupid,*" he told himself.

When Teddy couldn't fall back to sleep, he turned his lamp on again and reached for his *War Games Strategy Book*. He'd read barely a page when he found that he had little interest in it. The events of his dream were too vivid in his mind. Too *real*! But of course, it *had* to have been a dream. The weirdness that he'd thought had carried him through time and to places halfway around the world had just been an invention of his dreaming brain. *Hadn't it?*

Teddy put the book on his bedside table, turned off the lamp and closed his eyes. He tried to recall everything he'd seen and heard in his dream, playing it back like a movie. He wanted to see if, by reviewing it rationally, he could make any sense of it. This time, Teddy did nod off. Surrounded by the darkness and quiet of his own room and nestled in the soft warmth of his own bed, he heard the voice of the old veteran.

"You showed true courage in the plane, Teddy."

"No, I didn't," Teddy replied. "Anybody can be brave in a dream. It wasn't real."

"Wasn't it?" asked the voice.

Faces suddenly appeared, just as Teddy recalled them: Joe and Tom, A.J., Lieutenant Gordon, Commander Steele, Mel, Captain Bidwell and others.

"You didn't finish the poem," the voice said. "They need you to say the last line, Teddy. Say it with me. You remember where you left off in the plane? We shall not sleep . . ."

"Yes, I remember," Teddy said. Together with the voice, he recited, "We shall not sleep, though poppies grow, in Flanders fields."

The faces faded away into darkness, and the voice into silence.

Teddy arrived at school promptly at nine o'clock. Ms. Potts took attendance, and the students lined up to board the school bus. Valerie sat between Teddy and Paul on the long seat at the very back. As the bus pulled out of the school parking lot, Paul asked, "You all ready for the big game, Tedder? Gonna bombard the competition so they don't know what hit 'em?"

"Quiet down, you bonehead!" Valerie whispered. "You want Ms. Potts to hear?" She rolled her eyes and huffed.

"Oh, she can't hear me," Paul said dismissively. "She's way up at the front. So Teddy, have you cooked up a good story just in case you get caught?"

"I won't get caught," Teddy replied.

"You will," Valerie said in a harsh, sharp whisper. "Because it's a stupid idea."

Teddy said, "No, I won't. Because I'm not going to do it. I'm going to watch the Remembrance Day ceremony with you guys."

"WHAT?" Paul cried.

Valerie jabbed Paul with her elbow and again told him to quiet down. She smiled and gave a little wave and a shrug when Ms. Potts turned in her seat and fixed them with a "What's going on back there?" look. Then, when an outbreak of rambunctious behaviour elsewhere in the bus caught the teacher's attention, Valerie said, "Teddy! You've changed your mind about War Games?"

"Yeah, I guess I did," Teddy said.

"But why?" Paul asked. "You had it all worked out. It was brilliant."

Valerie jabbed Paul with her elbow again.

"Ow!" said Paul.

"Why, Teddy?" asked Valerie.

Teddy had considered telling his friends all about the dream but decided not to — at least, not just now.

"I guess because you were right, Val," he said. "It was a stupid idea."

Valerie didn't roll her eyes. She didn't huff. She didn't say a word. She just leaned over and gave Teddy a little peck on the cheek.

Teddy felt his heart flutter. Paul said, "Woo-oo!" Valerie

jabbed Paul again. When the bus pulled into the arena parking lot a few minutes later, the War Games competition was
the furthest thing from Teddy's mind.

The arena was packed, with students making up half of
the audience. Even so, from their seats in a section opposite
to where Teddy sat, his parents spotted him. He saw them
wave at him, and he waved back. He was glad he wouldn't
have to lie to them.

The ice surface had been covered with plywood boarding,
and a memorial to the war dead had been placed in the centre. Cadets representing the three branches of the Canadian
Armed Forces stood around it as an honour guard. On one
side, rows of chairs awaited city officials, guest speakers and
all of the people — military and civilian — who marched or
walked in a procession that emerged through a gate ordi-
narily used by hockey players.

The cavernous interior resounded with the wail of bagpipes accompanied by drums and horns as a marching band
in Scottish regalia led the procession. It included cadets, military personnel, police officers, firefighters, Boy Scouts and
Girl Guides. Last in the long line that wound around the
arena were the senior war veterans, wearing their uniforms
and medals.

There weren't many of them. Some walking, some using
wheelchairs guided by assistants, the veterans proudly entered the arena. Teddy picked out Mr. Sanderson among
them. The audience rose to applaud the old soldiers and then

remained standing for the singing of "O Canada" and "God Save the Queen."

The mayor and other officials and dignitaries made solemn speeches. People laid wreaths decorated with poppies at the base of the monument. The audience joined a high school choir in a musical version of "In Flanders Fields."

Teddy had heard the song at previous Remembrance Day ceremonies. He's always thought it was dull. But now the words filled his head with memories and images of the veteran and his poppy and all the events of the night before.

At eleven o'clock, a hush fell over the audience as one and all observed a minute of silence in homage to the war dead. Then the arena boomed, and babies and small children cried when soldiers fired the traditional 21-gun salute.

The ceremony was in many ways identical to Remembrance Day observances Teddy had attended with his class in previous years, events he had just a day earlier dismissed as boring and pointless. The proceedings were indeed the same, but Teddy had changed. Everything that had happened since that first strange moment in Mr. Singh's store paraded through his mind. Terrible things that he'd seen and heard! But most profoundly, people he'd met — or, rather, *dreamed* he'd met.

Among the people sitting in the rows of chairs were relatives of war victims whose names were on the city cenotaph. Teddy didn't know them personally, but he nonetheless felt he shared a bond with them because of Joe. And in spite of insisting to himself that dreams were dreams and nothing more, he still wondered about the fates of A.J. and Mel. Should he have *not* recited the poem but allowed himself to dream a little longer? Teddy decided that was silly and tried to shake it off. It slipped into a corner of his mind and didn't really go away. He kept thinking about War Games, which was fun but wasn't real, and real war, which was no fun at all for the people who were caught up in it.

On the bus taking them back to school, Valerie asked, "So, do you guys know what you're going to say in your essays?"

"Yeah," Paul replied. "I'm going to write about how Teddy came up with a master plan to sneak out and go to the War Games —"

This time Valerie couldn't jab Paul with her elbow, because he'd taken the precaution of sitting on the other side of Teddy. Instead, Teddy grabbed the peak of Paul's cap and pulled it down over his face at the same moment that Valerie said, "Bonehead!"

"Hey!" Paul exclaimed. "Only kidding! I'm going to write about exactly what happened. First, we sat down, then there was a procession, then we sang 'O Canada' and 'God Save the Queen,' then there were speeches, then I farted, then . . ."

"Double bonehead!" Valerie said. "Well, *I'm* going to write about how Remembrance Day is important because it reminds us that people die in wars and peace is always better."

"That sounds very nerdy," said Paul. He made a big, fake yawn and said, "Valerie will probably get an A, as usual. What about you, Tedder?"

"I'm not sure what I'll write about," Teddy said. "I'm still thinking about it. I might have to do a bit of research."

Back at home, Teddy had lunch with his father while his mother was out doing errands. He had questions about some of the things he'd dreamed, but he didn't want to say anything to his dad about dreams and the weirdness because it might sound crazy. Instead, he said, "Dad, I have to write a Remembrance Day essay for school. Valerie is going to write something about war and peace that will probably be brilliant."

"Just like Leo Tolstoy?" Dad asked.

"I don't know him. He's not in our class," said Teddy. "And Paul is going to write something boneheaded."

"Just like Paul," said Dad.

"I want to write about our family," Teddy said. "But I need some information. Can you help me?"

"Glad to, Ted. Any way I can," Dad looked as pleased as could be. "What would you like to know?"

Teddy said, "Remember last night when you and Mom were showing me pictures and medals and telling me about all the people in our family who were in wars? Well, what happened when . . ."

To his father's surprise, Teddy became a fountain of questions. Some were about family lore, and Dad answered those as best he could. But others were more difficult.

"We need to do some historical research," Dad said. "Let's see what we can find on the internet."

"When Ms. Potts gives us history projects, she tells us to go to the library and get books for research," Teddy said. "She says the internet is helpful, but it doesn't have everything, and a lot of the information people put on it isn't accurate."

"I agree with Ms. Potts," Dad replied. "But some of the books and documents we need for this project aren't likely to be in our local library. However, there are probably some reliable websites we can investigate."

They went up to Teddy's room and turned on his computer. Dad pulled up a chair in front of it, and Teddy sat on his bed. After searching for a few minutes, Dad found a website for Library and Archives Canada that had the attestation forms and other documents for all the soldiers of the Canadian Expeditionary Force of World War I. He entered the name "Thomas Nugent." Soon, to Teddy's excitement, he was looking at an image of Tom's attestation form, the very document he had filled out on the day he enlisted.

Dad printed it. Teddy held it in his hands, his eyes fixed on the signature Tom had put on the bottom of the sheet over a hundred years ago. He couldn't help but wonder if Tom had any real idea of what he was getting into when he signed that paper. Then he thought, *None of them did.*

Teddy said, "This is great, Dad. Let's find Joe's."

"You mean Uncle Joseph," Dad said.

"Oh, yes," Teddy said. "I didn't mean any disrespect. It's just that . . . um . . . in the picture, he looks so young — like a guy who'd say, 'Call me Joe.'"

Dad found Joe's attestation form. He also found the Circumstance of Casualty card that had the official report on Joe's death. It simply said, "Killed in action at Vimy Ridge."

"Sure doesn't say much, does it?" Dad said. "This is the first time I've seen these documents, Ted. I didn't know until now that Uncle Joseph died at Vimy Ridge."

Teddy thought the report was coldly brief, too. It didn't say anything about Joe's bravery. But seeing the words *Vimy Ridge* stunned him. Teddy hadn't known any more than his father that Joe had been killed in that battle. But in his dream ... Was it just a coincidence? Then he remembered that shortly before he'd gone to bed, Dad had asked him if he wanted to watch a documentary about Vimy Ridge. *That* must have been why it got into his dream!

"Okay, Ted, let's see if we can find anything on David Steele, *your* great-grandfather on *my* mother's side," Dad said. "You know, this has me thinking that we ought to keep digging and draw up a family tree. Might be interesting, eh, buddy?"

Teddy agreed. But at the moment he was anxious to see if there would be any other "coincidences."

Teddy was very adept on a computer, and Dad knew where to look for the information they wanted. Together they searched numerous websites with links to documents concerning Royal Canadian Navy ships and personnel of World War II. It took a while. Previously, Teddy would have had little patience with such painstaking work for a school project. But now he was looking for information he *wanted* to know.

"Found him!" Dad cried triumphantly. "Commander David Steele of HMCS *Wolverine*, a corvette."

Once again, Teddy was startled. *Wolverine*! The ship in his dream! He hadn't known the names of *any* World War II ships, except the German battleship *Bismarck*. He'd once started to watch an old black and white movie about that ship with his father but hadn't watched it for long because he thought that whole business of war at sea looked pretty boring. Not at all like the fast-paced outer space battles in *Star Wars* movies.

So why did the ship in his dream have the right name? There *had* to be a sensible reason. Teddy thought he had one.

Superhero Wolverine, of the X-Men, was Canadian. Maybe that's why his dreaming brain came up with that name for a Canadian ship. That idea seemed a bit of a stretch, but it was the only logical explanation Teddy could come up with.

But another word Dad used threatened to shoot down that idea. *Corvette!* How had his dreaming brain known that the ship was a corvette? The only corvette Teddy had ever heard of before was a sports car. Had he once read a comic book in which Wolverine drove one?

"The *Wolverine* was part of a convoy escort in the North Atlantic," Dad said, reading from a page on the computer screen. "The convoy was attacked by a U-boat wolf pack. Six ships were sunk by torpedoes, including the *Wolverine*. Commander Steele and most of the crew survived the sinking. This is really interesting, Ted. I knew my grandfather survived a sinking, but I didn't know the name of the ship or the circumstances."

Teddy instantly forgot about Wolverine of the X-Men. "Most?" he said. "Does it say who *didn't* survive?"

Teddy wasn't sure what he was more afraid of: hearing that A.J. had died, or hearing A.J.'s name at all. Because he couldn't think of a single reason, not even a far-fetched one, for his dreaming imagination to have come up with the name of a real person who had been aboard the real *Wolverine*.

Dad scrolled down through the blocks of text. "It says that three of the *Wolverine's* men were lost. Two who were working in the engine room when the torpedo exploded and a gunner who was thrown overboard. It doesn't give their names."

Now Teddy's mind was spinning. The gunner! *Morgan!* He was *real*! And if Morgan was real, was A.J., too? The A.J. in his dream didn't work in the engine room, so he couldn't have been one of the two sailors who were killed there. Teddy was glad A.J. had survived and sorry that three men hadn't. But things still didn't fit.

Teddy had known nothing about the sinking of the *Wolverine* before he dreamed it. Now he wrestled with yet another mystery. Shouldn't the report say that the *Wolverine* lost *four* crew members? *He* had been thrown overboard, too, and then left behind. Or at least, he'd dreamed he had. Teddy had heard about people having dreams that came true, like peeks into the future. Was it possible to have dreams that were peeks into the past? Could a memory of that event have been passed down to him from Commander Steele in some sort of psychic DNA? It was all just too mystifying.

As Teddy's mind whirled, he felt certain of just one thing. The account of the *Wolverine*'s sinking said three men were lost, not four. That meant that however close his dream had been to the actual story, *he* hadn't really been there. It would be foolish for him to think otherwise.

"You okay, Ted?" Dad asked. "You're not getting bored already, are you?"

"What? Oh, sorry," Teddy responded. "I was just thinking that we're finding some pretty cool stuff about our family. What about the bomber pilot who Mom said won a medal?"

"Ah, yes! Old Harry Bidwell!" Dad said. "Distinguished Flying Cross. Let's see if we can find him."

They investigated websites and links. They heard Mom come in, and when she called out to them, Teddy answered, "We're up here."

At last, Dad said, "Here's a website made by a Royal Air Force historian who collected first-hand stories from veterans who'd flown for Bomber Command during the Second World War. He recorded the interviews, and . . . hey, look at this, Ted! One of the interviews describes the incident for which Captain Harry Bidwell was awarded the Distinguished

Flying Cross. Your mother will want to hear this! After all, it's about her grandfather."

"*Yeah,*" Teddy said to himself. "*I want to hear it, too — I think.*"

A couple of minutes later, Mom was sitting on Teddy's bed. "This is very exciting," she said. "I knew Granddad was a war hero, but I've never known exactly what he did, because my mum and dad said he didn't like to talk about the war. Click on it, Teddy."

An image came on the computer screen of a group of men in RAF uniforms posing for a photograph in front of a Lancaster bomber. Mom got up to take a closer look.

"There he is," she said, pointing to the man in the middle. "That's Granddad."

Teddy took a closer look, too. Sure enough, the man Mom pointed to was the Captain Bidwell of his dream. All of the men's names were written at the bottom of the photograph: Albert King, Henry Platt, Martin Halliday, Harry Bidwell, David Jones, Daniel Johnson and . . . Melvin Lynn!

Teddy didn't have to read the names. He recognized all but one of the faces. So, Mel and all the others had been real, just like Tom and Joe, and A.J. But what about Daniel Johnson? Who was he?

Then Teddy remembered. In his dream, Mel had said that "poor 'ol Danny boy" had fallen ill with food poisoning. Teddy was his last-minute replacement. The photograph had obviously been taken sometime before Danny got sick. As

Teddy tried to untangle thoughts and explanations that seemed to solve nothing, a familiar voice came from his computer's speakers.

"I was the wireless operator and nose gunner in a Lanc under the command of Captain 'arry Bidwell. And a loverly bloke 'e was."

The voice was that of an older man, but Teddy knew it was Mel.

"We was part of a bombin' raid on the Nazi U-boat pens in Boulogne, in France. Tryin' to 'elp out the navy lads by strikin' the wolf packs right in their lair. We 'ad Jerry night-fighters all over us, and the flack was as thick as flies around a jar of me auntie's jam. We got our bombs away all right. A nice little gift for 'itler."

"Now that's a Cockney accent if I ever heard one," Dad said.

"Shhh! Just listen," Mom whispered as the story continued.

"We turned for 'ome but 'adn't gone far before the Jerries got us. Our plane was shot up like an 'awk over an 'en 'ouse. Our tail gunner, a chap named Jones, was killed in his turret. I was 'it, too. I don't remember nothin' that 'appened after that. I can only tell you what was told to me later, in the 'ospital."

Teddy and his parents heard the voice of the interviewer ask, "And what were you told, Sergeant Lynne?"

"Oh, blimey!" came the response. "I ain't been a sergeant for over fifty flippin' years. Just call me Mel."

"Very well," said the interviewer. "Tell me what happened, Mel."

"Well, according to what I 'eard later, the plane was goin' down over water. Biddy . . . Captain Bidwell was tryin' to keep 'er aloft long enough for everyone to bail out. 'E wasn't goin' to leave the controls until every crew member that was still alive was out the escape 'atch. So they all jumped. They thought I was dead, you see."

At that point, Mel's voice became choked with emotion.

"Sorry, mate," he said when he'd recovered himself. "I ain't talked about this in years. Still gets to me, you know."

"In your own good time, Mel," the interviewer said.

"The lads all bailed out," Mel said. "They 'ad to, you see. No other choice. I mean, what would you do, mate? Anyway, Captain Bidwell would 'ave followed 'em. But 'e 'eard *me*! I wasn't dead after all, you see. Biddy 'eard moans and mumbles and knew I was alive. I was told 'e even 'eard me say 'Cheerio,' like I was sayin' goodbye to somebody.

"Well, Captain 'arry Bidwell, bless 'is 'eart, wasn't about to bail out and leave one of 'is lads. Biddy stayed at the controls. By skill and flippin' magic, 'e managed to belly-land that plane on the water."

"He *did* it!" Teddy gasped. "That plane was . . ."

Both parents *shushed* him. Teddy was immediately glad of that. He'd been about to say something he couldn't possibly explain.

"Like I said," Mel continued, "I 'ave no memory of this

meself. Captain Bidwell found me unconscious. I was 'alfway out of me turret. If I 'adn't been, 'e might not 'ave got me out before the plane sank. I guess me guardian angel was with me. Biddy got me into a dinghy, and in the morning we got rescued by a Royal Navy destroyer."

Teddy held back the urge to pump his fist in the air and shout, "YES!"

"That's the story, mate," Mel said. "Captain Bidwell got a medal, and 'e deserved it, 'e did. But all those other lads were 'eros, too. Me and Biddy and 'enry Platt were the only ones from that crew still alive when the war was over. The lads that didn't make it, well, their names are on war memorials. My name would be there, too, if it wasn't for Captain Bidwell."

The recording ended.

For a few moments, Teddy and his parents sat in silence. Then Dad said, "That was an amazing story."

"It certainly was," Mom agreed. "What makes me proud is knowing that Granddad was awarded that medal, not for dropping bombs but for risking his own life to save someone else. Save that link for me, please, Teddy, because I've got to share it with the rest of the family. I'll bet they don't even know it exists."

Dad said, "Well, Ted, your mother and I have learned some things because of *your* project. But how about you? Has our little research session helped?"

"Yeah," Teddy replied. "Something that man, Mel, said gave me an idea. There are real stories behind the names on war memorials. I was going to write about *our* family, but now my topic is going to be about how all of the people who died in the wars left behind families."

But even as Teddy spoke, questions about what he'd just heard ran through his mind. If Mel, Captain Bidwell and Henry Platt were the only ones who survived the war, what had happened to the others? Were they all killed in action, like David Jones? Teddy hadn't liked Lieutenant King very much, but he was still sorry to learn that he'd died.

Of course, he didn't know what Lieutenant King was really like; the Lieutenant King he'd known was only a figure in a dream. But what about Captain Bidwell saying he heard Mel say "Cheerio"? That's what Mel said to Teddy in his dream. But *everybody* knew British people said "Cheerio."

How did the wounded, unconscious Mel pull himself halfway out of his turret? Could one of the other crewmen have been his "guardian angel?" No! They wouldn't have just left him there. Who manned the plane's dorsal gun turret in the absence of Daniel Johnson? Maybe one of the other crewmen had done double duty. Or maybe Danny was actually on that mission and had only been on sick leave in Teddy's dream.

The more Teddy thought about the recording, the more bewildering it was. How could he have dreamed details he couldn't have known about that flight before hearing the interview? Nonetheless, he told himself firmly that he hadn't *really* been on that plane, just as he hadn't really been on the *Wolverine* or in the trenches.

As questions flew through Teddy's mind, Mom noticed something on Teddy's pillow.

"Where did you get this pillowcase, Teddy?" she asked.

"What?" said Teddy, snapping out of his puzzle of thoughts. "My pillowcase?"

He looked and was amazed to see that the poppy he'd pinned to his pillowcase — the poppy the old veteran had given him — was no longer there. In its place was a bright red, black-centred poppy *embroidered* into his pillowcase. It stood out against the white fabric like a badge — or a medal.

Teddy was at a loss for words. He suspected — *knew* — it had something to do with the veteran, actually his great-grandfather, and with his dream, with the weirdness. But how could he explain that to his parents? He didn't want to make up a lie, and he wasn't even sure what was true.

Then Dad said, "It looks like a pretty nice Remembrance Day memento."

"Yes, isn't it?" Teddy said quickly. "I got it yesterday from a veteran who was selling poppies in front of Mr. Singh's store. He said it was special."

"That was kind of him," said Mom. "I hope you said thank you."

"I did," Teddy said. Inside, he sighed with relief. He hadn't said a word of a lie. But he was still astonished at the sight of the poppy.

Mom ran her fingers over the embroidered poppy. Then she picked up the pillow so she could examine it more closely.

Something that had been under the pillow caught her eye. Teddy and Dad saw it, too, and Teddy suppressed a gasp. It was an egg.

Mom picked it up and said, "Teddy! A hard-boiled egg under your pillow! What have I told you about snacks in bed?"

Teddy said, "Sorry."

Then he thought again about his dream; of Tom and Joe; and A.J. and the *Wolverine*; and Mel, Captain Bidwell and the rest of the crew of the Lancaster, and he wondered. In his mind, he repeated the poem, "In Flanders Fields." He knew that the four most important words in his essay would be, "Loved and were loved."

ACKNOWLEDGEMENTS

The author would like to thank Ronsdale Press and
everyone who contributed to the preparation of this
book for publication: Kevin Welsh, Wendy Atkinson,
Robyn So, and special thanks to the late Ron Hatch.
Thanks also to the staff of the Guelph Public Library
and to John Robert Colombo.

Many books have been written about Canada's involvement in the World Wars and about the experiences of people who served in the armed forces. Readers might like to explore these titles:

- *Desperate Glory: The Story of WWI*, by John Wilson, Napoleon Publishing

- *For King & Empire: The Canadians at Vimy, April 1917*, by Norm Christie, CEF Books

- *Victory at Vimy: Canada Comes of Age, April 9–12, 1917*, by Ted Barris, T. Allen Publishers

- *Corvettes Canada: Convoy Veterans of World War II Tell Their True Stories*, by Mac Johnston, Wiley and Sons Canada

- *The Royal Air Force 1939–1945*, by Chaz Bowyer, Hamlyn Publishing Group

- *This Withering Disease of Conflict: A Canadian Soldier's Chronicle of the First World War*, by Edward Butts (a collection of the wartime letters and articles written by journalist Herbert Philp), Guelph Historical Society

ABOUT THE AUTHOR

Ed Butts's list of books written for both adult and young readers includes titles that have been nominated for the Arthur Ellis Award, the Red Maple Award and the Hackmatack Award. His book *Wartime: The First World War in a Canadian Town* won the Ontario Historical Society's J.J. Talman Award. *This Game of War* was inspired by the author's research into the stories behind the names on the cenotaph in his hometown of Guelph, Ontario, and by his annual attendance at the Remembrance Day ceremonies there.